All rights reserved. No part of this book may be reproduced in any form by any electronic or mechanical means including photocopying, recording, or information storage and retrieval without permission in writing from the author.

The Business Plan Copyright © 2016 Lorhainne Ekelund
The Business Plan Paperback Copyright © 2021 Lorhainne Ekelund
Editor: Talia Leduc

All rights reserved.
ISBN-13: 978-1990590443

Give feedback on the book at:
lorhainneeckhart@hotmail.com

Twitter: @LEckhart
Facebook: AuthorLorhainneEckhart

Printed in the U.S.A

THE BUSINESS PLAN

THE FRIESSENS (NEIL & CANDY)

LORHAINNE ECKHART

The Outsider Series

The Forgotten Child (Brad and Emily)
A Baby and a Wedding
Fallen Hero (Andy, Jed, and Diana)
The Search
The Awakening (Andy and Laura)
Secrets (Jed and Diana)
Runaway (Andy and Laura)
Overdue
The Unexpected Storm (Neil and Candy)
The Wedding (Neil and Candy)

The Friessens: A New Beginning

The Deadline (Andy and Laura)
The Price to Love (Neil and Candy)
A Different Kind of Love (Brad and Emily)
A Vow of Love, A Friessen Family Christmas

The Friessens

The Reunion
The Bloodline (Andy & Laura)
The Promise (Diana & Jed)

The Friessens Family

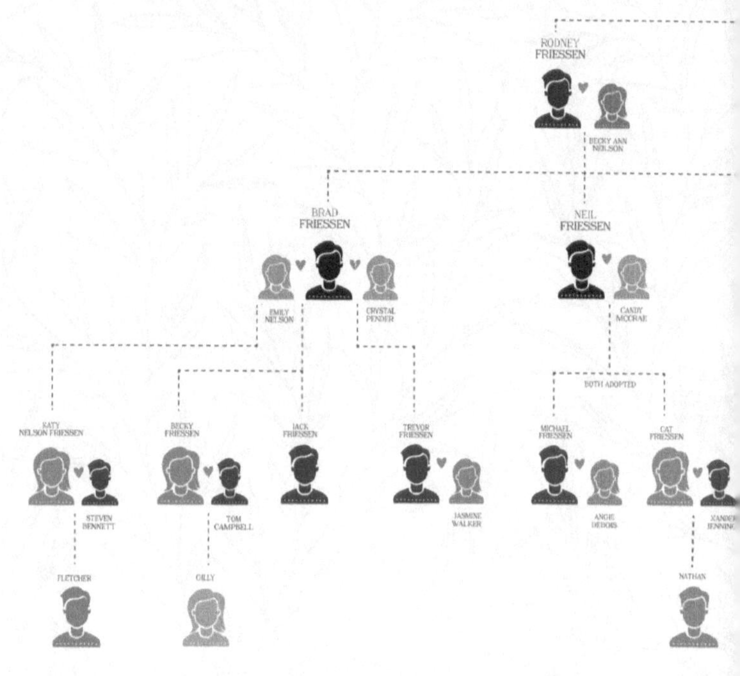

The Outsider

THE FORGOTTEN CHILD	BRAD & EMILY
A BABY AND A WEDDING	BRAD & EMILY & *the great Jed, Neil Rodney & Becky*
FALLEN HERO	JED, DIANA & ANDY
THE SEARCH	JED, DIANA & ANDY
THE AWAKENING	ANDY & LAURA

The Outsider

SECRETS	DIANA & JED *with the entire Friessen Family*
RUNAWAY	ANDY & LAURA
OVERDUE	JED & DIANA
THE UNEXPECTED STORM	NEIL & CANDY
THE WEDDING	NEIL & CANDY *and the entire Friessen Family*

The Friessens: A New Beginning

THE DEADLINE	ANDY & LAURA
THE PRICE TO LOVE	NEIL & CANDY
A DIFFERENT KIND OF LOVE	BRAD & EMILY
A VOW OF LOVE	THE ENTIRE
A FRIESSEN FAMILY CHRISTMAS	FRIESSEN FAMILY

The Friessens

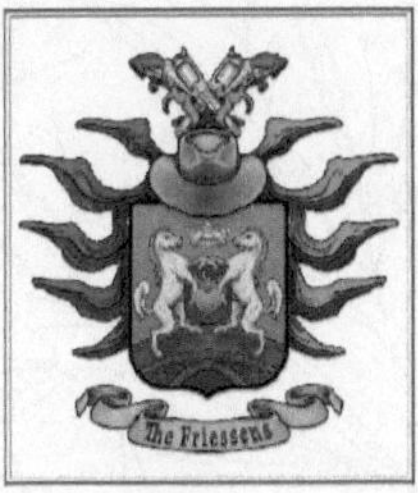

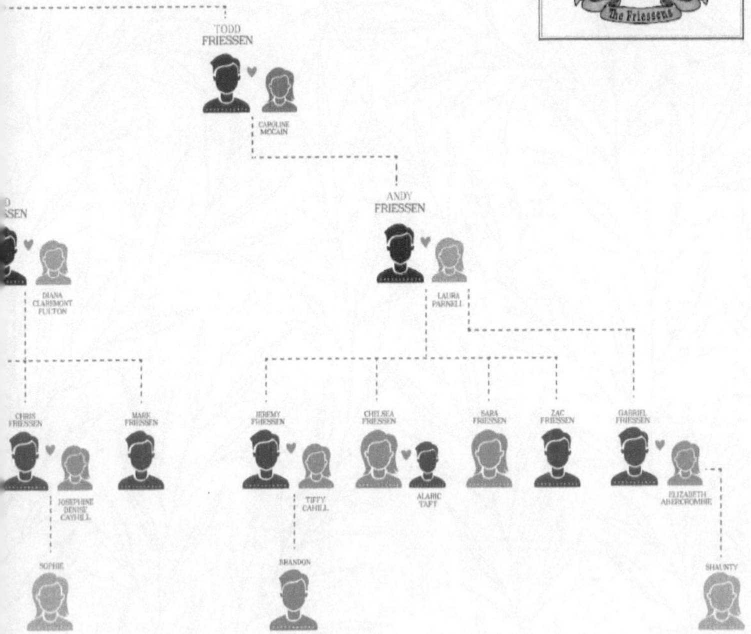
TODD FRIESSEN
CAROLINE MCCAIN
ANDY FRIESSEN
LAURA PARNELL
DIANA CLAREMONT FULTON
CHRIS FRIESSEN
MARK FRIESSEN
JOSEPHINE DENISE CAYHILL
SOPHIE
JEREMY FRIESSEN
TIFFY CAHILL
BRANDON
CHELSEA FRIESSEN
ALARIC TAFT
SARA FRIESSEN
ZAC FRIESSEN
GABRIEL FRIESSEN
ELIZABETH ABERCROMBIE
SHAUNTY

THE ENTIRE FRIESSEN FAMILY
ANDY & LAURA
JED & DIANA
NEIL & CANDY
BRAD & EMILY
KATY & STEVEN
KATY & STEVEN

The Friessens

LEAVE THE LIGHT ON	KATY & STEVEN
IN THE MOMENT	BECKY & TOM *introducing you to a new character Vic McCabe which then launches a new series The McCabe Brothers*
IN THE FAMILY *A Friessen Family Christmas*	THE ENTIRE FRIESSEN FAMILY
IN THE SILENCE	CAT & XANDER
IN THE STARS	DANNY & EVIE
IN THE CHARM	CHRIS & J.D.
UNEXPECTED CONSEQUENCES	CHRIS & J.D. *and Danny & Evie*

The Friessens

IT WAS ALWAYS YOU	KATY & STEVEN
THE FIRST TIME I SAW YOU	GABRIEL & ELIZABETH
WELCOME TO MY ARMS	CHELSEA & ALARIC
WELCOME TO BOSTON	PAIGE & MORGAN
I'LL ALWAYS LOVE YOU	JEREMY
GROUND RULES	JEREMY & TIFFY
A REASON TO BREATHE	TREVOR
YOU ARE MY EVERYTHING	MICHAEL

"A great read that is full of all those wonderful alpha Friessen men and the families they love. The emotions run high and the story is intense."

— AHERMAN

"I have read every book by this author, The Friessens are my favorite. But Neil is the one that always upset me the most. His attitude and the way he treated Candy, but I really loved him in this book. You need to get this book and read it and fall in love with this family & this author as I have."

— D. TAYLOR, REVIEWER

"This story of Candy and Neil is one you won't want to put down till the end. I think Neil is the least likable of the brothers and cousins, but he just may be the most interesting!"

— DEBBIE

Neil Friessen has almost everything he's ever wanted:

- His wife, the woman he's always loved…
- His children, whom he never believed he would have…
- And an empty bank account.

Until one day, that is, when he comes up with the business plan.

CHAPTER 1

"What did you do?" Candy said. She wasn't sure exactly what she was looking at when she took in her husband, Neil. His dark hair had once been short and impeccably groomed but was now curling around his ears and the back, brushing his shoulders. He also had a beard going on, and if truth be told, if someone asked her what she really thought about his new badass transformation, she would have to admit it was beginning to grow on her. She was thankful he had at least kept the beard trimmed, though, and hadn't took it upon himself to grow a pair of chops—because those would have to go.

"Do you like it?" He was dressed in a faded pair of jeans and a black T-shirt that was looking a little worn as he pulled off a pair of shades and tucked them in his shirt-front. A gleaming diamond stud sparkled in the light within his newly pierced left earlobe.

She just stared at her hunk of a husband, who was far too good looking for his own good. He had everything going for him: He was smart, sexy, and confident, with linebacker shoulders, six-pack abs, and full red lips that had tasted every inch of her. He was her lover, her husband, and the only man to ever have stirred her passion.

He raised his eyebrows, and his whiskey-colored eyes were filled with teasing and amusement. They were always filled with such confidence, such mystery, and were so intense that she could get lost in them forever. "It's my new look. Seriously, don't you like it?"

She couldn't help the laugh that bubbled out of her. "One, yes, I do—but, Neil, seriously? You're the most conservative man, or you were, who has ever graced my presence. Where the hell is my husband, and what have you done with him?"

She was holding Michael, who was now walking and into everything, and he even pointed at the tiny jewel in Neil's ear. "Dada," he said, pointing, his other hand on her shoulder, grabbing a fistful of her shirt.

"Yes, Daddy got an earring," Neil said, making a playful face to Michael, who laughed and reached out to him, leaning his little body so Candy had no choice but to pass him over.

Neil lifted his son, who was looking more and more like him every day, up high and then brought him down and kissed his cheek. The man was positively gaga over his children, Michael and Cat, the little deaf girl they had adopted in Mexico. Both adored him, and everything he did was for them.

"So what brought on this need to get an earring?" She had noticed Neil slipping into this change, becoming someone different—not the man she'd married but an evolution, someone trying to become someone else. He was charming, fun, loving, and still possessive, which she doubted would ever change, but she saw the changes in him every day. He listened to her now, and at the same time she couldn't help sensing him slipping, as if he were lost, trying to find his footing and searching for who he was. She frowned, or maybe he'd noticed where her thoughts had gone, as he furrowed his brow and looked deeply at her.

"What?" He made a face at Michael again before pretending to take a bite of him. Michael giggled, a full-bellied laugh that filled Candy with such joy.

"I'm starting to get a little worried about you, Neil."

His expression told her she was being ridiculous. He was trying to shake her off. "I'm the last person you should be worrying about. Seriously, over an earring? I thought you'd like it," he said.

"It's not just the earring, which I have to admit I kind of like. It's this change in you, as if you're transforming into your evil twin." She held her hand out to stop him when she knew he was about to lay into her, probably with some line about how she was misreading everything again and this was him changing to be a better man for her. "Seriously, Neil, I know how hard you've tried for me. You told me you were going to change, and I've watched you over the last year, how you've gone out of your way to put me and the children first. You stopped pushing and demanding and organizing—no, wait! You haven't stopped. You've toned it down some, which I appreciate, but..." She held up her hand again when he opened his mouth to say something. "I have the floor. Let me finish, please." She tapped his arm.

He gestured between them and then wrapped both his arms around Michael, holding him on his hip. "Please, by all means, lay it all out there."

"You sold the resort for me."

"Sale isn't final yet," he added rather matter of factly, as if she needed reminding.

"Okay, it's in the works is what I meant to say. Your dream…you walked away from it for me."

When he looked at her that way, he gave all of himself. It could be so disconcerting at times, but she knew he was taking all of what she was saying in, as if he were listening with every one of his senses. She was sure that was what had made him such a success in business.

"You've moved us way up here, about as far away from Cancun as we can get, and I'm not complaining. I find it rather nice, being this close to Emily and Brad, and the kids have their cousins close by, even though the cold and damp here is something I'm still trying to get used to. But, Neil, for the last while you've seemed to be floundering, as if you don't have any idea what it is you want to do. That's what's causing me some concern. It's this." She gestured to his earring. "When you walk out the door and say you need to run an errand, I don't know who's going to walk back through it or what idea you've come up with to be your new project here. Last I looked, you have the deck you still need to build, a patio half started, and, oh yeah, then there's the corral, the shed for my horse, and the pasture you keep telling me you're going to fence off so I can have my horse and donkey there instead of having to run over to Brad and Emily's all the time. The thing is, it's all great and everything, but you haven't finished one thing here."

Neil frowned and glanced at Michael, taking in his expression, his face, as if studying him, then looked back over to Candy. She wondered for a moment whether she'd hit a nerve. After all, the Friessen men had their pride, and she was pretty sure Neil's had taken a hammering.

"Maybe there are days I wonder, too," he said. "Trying to figure out what to do…I had my entire life planned out and saw everything happening one way, and then this curveball had me scrambling like I never had before. I get it, it's all on me. I screwed up big time, all because of my need to make things happen a certain way. This other stuff here, I really will finish it. There's just so much, and spending time with these guys…" He made another face at Michael and kissed his chubby cheeks, and Michael giggled and patted at him.

He looked over at Candy with such intensity she had to hold her breath. "But we can't control things, life. It's the other way around. And once you realize you have no control, it's amazing, this feeling of freedom that happens." His eyes simmered with warmth, with love, which had her heart flip flopping.

She was resting her hand on her chest at the open V of her light sweater, skimming over the bare skin, thinking of what this was with him. At times, Neil took her breath away, and at times, like this, he left her speechless. She was about to say something more, but this evolved Neil had Candy scrambling, her mind blanking. At the same time, she was freaking out, wondering what the next transformation for Neil Friessen was going to be.

"Maybe you should call Brad. Maybe this new and improved Neil could use some grounding from his big brother, help you get your head on straight and focused in one direction." She stepped forward and reached for Michael, who went easily into her arms. "Come on, baby. Time for lunch."

When she glanced back at Neil, what she saw was him checking out his image in the hall mirror, taking in his look. On second thought, maybe it would be a better idea if she called Brad herself.

CHAPTER 2

Neil was digging post holes at the back of the house so he could put in the rails and finish the corral he was building for Candy's horse, Sable, the gray Azteca he'd brought back from Cancun along with the floppy-eared donkey, Ambrose, whom she'd rescued from the side of the road as a baby. The donkey had now grown and was getting fatter by the minute along with Sable and the stable of other horses Brad currently had on his ranch, the family ranch. This was just one of the many projects he'd promised Candy he'd get to, and he knew he was leaving a trail of work left undone. The problem was that everything as of late wasn't filling him with that burning excitement he got when he was doing something he loved. Life was too short for him to be doing things that didn't interest him.

Maybe he'd also realized now that it was easier keeping the horse at Brad's. Since Neil and Candy had ended up driving twenty minutes to the ranch four times a week, he wasn't having to shovel up all the manure, feed and water them, and send them out to graze. Those were all just more things that didn't interest him. Working with animals, being part of the land was what drove his brothers, Jed and Brad, and even his cousin, Andy, with his herd of long-horns in Montana. Besides, they spent more and more time at Brad and Emily's, where Candy and Emily had taken to heading out for afternoons on the trail, of which there were tons on the public land Brad's ranch backed onto. Here, Candy would have to make do with just their fifteen-acre oceanfront. There was no other place to ride. Maybe he should reevaluate.

It was better riding a horse over at Brad's, with lots more places to explore. Neil had joined Candy and Emily twice, but after that he'd decided to hang back with the kids, giving Candy and Emily some girl time alone. They were becoming fast friends, and even though Neil enjoyed being with his wife all the time, he had to remind himself she needed space. It was his hovering and obsessive need to know where she was and everything she was doing that had started to come between them.

That was something he'd once done, trying to control everything about her. He had to remind himself it had come out of his love for her, out of him never wanting her to struggle as she had before. He loved her so much, and all he wanted was to make everything easier for her, but she was stronger than that, and sometimes he had to let go and let her stumble on her own, within reason, for their love to grow.

He'd promised to be more open, to stop pushing, controlling, and organizing, and to stop keeping his plans and dreams from her. He jammed the shovel in the ground, hitting a rock, and swore as he glanced back at the house again, where his wife was with Michael and Cat. He could see her in the window of the kitchen. She smiled and waved at him and gestured with a glass, holding it up. He nodded and watched as his wife opened the fridge and then, moments later, stepped outside onto the back deck. Cat walked out with her in a sweater and red leggings, and Candy smiled down at their little girl, who was turning six but had still not started school, as Candy said she wasn't ready. She gestured for Cat to follow as she walked over to Neil with a glass of water.

It was a sunny day for this early in the spring, not a cloud in the sky. He watched the confidence in his wife. She was dressed casually in blue jeans and a white tee, a cream sweater pulled overtop.

"Wow, can't believe how much you've done," she said.

His fingers touched Candy's as she handed him the cool glass. "Thank you," he said, then guzzled it down and wiped the water from his mouth with the back of his hand.

He was shirtless and sweaty from all the digging he'd been doing, and Candy didn't try to hide her interest or amusement.

"What?" he said when he noticed the teasing light in her eyes.

"Can't remember ever seeing you get your hands dirty, either. You're the one who's always hired help to do the grunt work." She smiled brightly. "I kind of like it."

The old Neil would have hated this, but there was something refreshing about all this back-breaking work that seemed to help him think through some of the nagging issues he'd been tossing around in his mind.

"You know how we talked about not keeping things from each other?" he said, noting the moment her eyes darkened and a hint of worry flickered there. He reached out and touched her arm, feeling her stiffen. He knew she was worried about what he'd done now. She took a moment, thankfully, and didn't pull away as Cat latched on to his leg, looking up with a bright smile, flashing her white baby teeth, her cochlear implant attached behind her ear.

"Daddy, play," she said, her voice flat. There was something about the way she looked at him, adored him, that could make him do anything for her. He reached down, his hands caked with dirt, and tickled her chin.

"Can't, baby girl. Got to finish this for Mommy."

"Please?" she said, holding his leg, bouncing on her toes.

He glanced over to Candy, who still appeared distracted as she smiled down at Cat and over to Neil in amusement.

"I'll tell you what. You let Daddy just talk to Mommy for a minute, and then I'm all yours. Meet you in the sandbox," he said and watched as Cat ran in her awkward way, slowly and unsteadily, to the small plastic square sandbox Neil had bought. "We need to get her balance checked, I think. Maybe we should put in a swing set, or maybe I could put together one of those giant backyard treehouses with a slide and swings and a teeter totter to give the kids something to really play on." He took in the cleared empty lot, which went for a long ways over to the bank that dropped off to the ocean, then glanced to Cat. "You know what? I think I need to put up a fence in the back to keep the kids in." When he looked over at Candy, her entire expression had changed as if she were trying to figure out what was going on in his head.

"Neil, that's an awful lot of projects you're planning. You haven't finished one thing you've started, and now you want to start something else. How about sticking to one task and finishing it?" She firmed her lips then. "Are you keeping secrets? Is there something else going on, something you need to tell me?" She had completely misunderstood. He didn't like seeing the worry that seemed to come over her so quickly, as if she were remembering how it used to be.

He shook his head. "No, I was kind of alluding to you, my dear wife." He gripped the handle of the shovel, squeezing, watching her expression, which went from shock to confusion. He gestured between them as he often did in business to get things moving. "So tell me, Candy, are there any secrets you'd maybe like to share with me?"

CHAPTER 3

He'd promised to give her space. He wouldn't push. Those had been his exact words to her after what had seemed to be the beginning of the end of their marriage. Neil had been so controlling about everything about their relationship, and his obsession had almost destroyed them. Over the past year, she'd watched him do everything in his power to change, to become a better man.

She was watching Neil from the deck, resting her hands on the railing as he ran with Cat across the backyard over the damp grass, both of them dirty and covered in mud. They were laughing and giggling, and Neil was now on the ground, tossing Cat in the air. She was laughing with such joy shining from her that it brought tears to Candy's eyes.

The happiness he provided their children had her heart filling up so full that at times she couldn't breathe, fearing her chest would burst. She loved Neil deeply, but there were times she wondered whether that was enough. He was an amazing father and an incredible lover, but there was still that gulf there where she'd always wonder if there was something more he was hiding from her. There was still that distance where he couldn't be her best friend. She knew he wanted that ultimate trust, that confidence, to know everything she was thinking and feeling.

He had created such a horrible lie, though. It had been so cruel that it had almost destroyed everything good because of his need for a child, a child that was his. Michael had come from a surrogate to whom, in the end, Neil had given everything he had so she would go away. He had been obsessed and had made the choice not to tell her who Michael really was until the letter had arrived in the mail from the surrogate, begging to see her son and Neil, with whom she'd fallen in love. That letter had sliced through her heart like a knife, gutting her. She had felt her entire marriage, world, and family fall away.

"Hey, what's with the heavy thoughts?" Neil was carrying a giggling dirt-covered little girl with rosy cheeks and a smile that should be on every child's face. Neil was just as messy, wearing his sweat-covered green striped T-shirt with ground-in dirt and grass stains. This was an image of her husband she'd never expected to see. He put Cat down. "Boots off. Go on in the house, baby. Daddy will be right there, and I'll get you cleaned up."

"Just thinking of things," Candy said.

Neil stepped closer and reached up, running his hand over her cheek and touching the side of her ear. "You were frowning, a look I've seen before when you're upset. Remember how we talked about no secrets, about talking, not hiding things from each other? But here you've been keeping a lot from me." He gestured, and she didn't miss the concern for her in his expression.

She crossed her arms, wondering what specifically he was talking about. "You've never asked to read my journal where I write everything down. Are you asking now?"

Would he push it like he would have when they were first married? Back then, he'd have opened the book and started reading anyway, believing he didn't have to ask permission, that it was his right. That had been Neil before their world had come crashing down, the obsessive Neil who had to know everything she was thinking, down to the point she lost everything about herself and who she was.

He had a shrewdness in his gaze at times, and he narrowed his eyes, the amber color deepening and reaching into her. The man had the ability to tip her emotions over, having her heart skipping a beat. "I'm not talking about your journal. That's yours, your private thoughts. You know already how I feel about that. I told you I'd never push, and I won't. You have to trust me. I won't cross that boundary. That would be up to you to feel comfortable enough to want to show it to me. You know how much I love you. Everything you're thinking, feeling, your hopes and dreams, everything that goes through your mind…I want to be the first and only person you want to share that with. I hope to get there, but you have to want that. You have to be ready."

He was touching her face again, sliding his thumb over her chin, her lips, as she stared at his wild, disheveled look. Her neat and tidy husband was turning into someone she didn't recognize, damn attractive and sexy, like a man who lived on the wild side of life.

"Then what are you talking about if not my journal?" What did he think she was keeping from him?

He pulled his hand away, lowering it to his side, and then glanced away as if thinking about what he should or shouldn't say. Of course she swallowed, wondering where his head was, what he thought she knew and hadn't shared.

"I've waited for you to say something to me for so long, and you never did. It's the one thing I can't understand you

not sharing with me, considering it was about my parents."
He was in her face, baring his teeth, and in that moment,
as she blinked, trying to absorb and understand his mean-
ing, she realized he'd learned the ugly truth. For the first
time in her life, Candy was feeling like the bad guy, having
kept from him the one thing she knew he would never
understand.

"You found out about your parents," she said. "How?"

CHAPTER 4

Michael had woken up from his nap before Candy could say another word. Her cheeks had flushed, and for a moment she had appeared uneasy, embarrassed, and tongue tied, which made absolutely no sense, considering he was the one man she should never feel any of those things with. How long had she been holding on to this secret for? He didn't know, and in some weird way, he couldn't help feeling as if she'd betrayed him.

Candy was upstairs now, changing Michael, and he listened to his boy as he slid down the carpeted stairs wearing just a pull-up and a T-shirt, his dark wavy hair touching his shoulders. His boy was also beginning to resemble him and take on his shaggy appearance.

"Hey there, you." He grabbed Michael and tossed him a bit as he laughed, breathing in that baby scent that still lingered.

"Neil, were you going to bathe Cat, or do you want me to?" Candy called out from upstairs. "And don't forget Brad, Emily, and the kids are coming for dinner tonight. It's our turn…" She was coming down the stairs, her hand on the railing, and she stopped and stared at him as if he weren't even listening to her, though the fact was that he'd never stopped.

"Run the bath for Cat. We'll toss this guy in, too. Then we need to talk," he said, this time not willing to let Candy off about not letting him in on the little bomb his parents had shared with her.

Maybe she knew, as she seemed to hesitate before looking up the stairs and back to him. Instead of putting up a wall or pushing back as she did at times, her expression seemed to give in just a bit as she nodded. "Okay, but remember you said you were putting the barbecue together, and I'm pretty sure it's still sitting in the box in pieces in the garage."

Who cares? he thought. Seriously, he'd use the stove. "Is this where you lay into me again about everything I have yet to do?" He rubbed his head, thinking of everything: the lawn mower still boxed, the patio with its bricks still under a tarp, the pile of sand around the corner that still needed to be laid out and raked and flattened. Then there was the front deck he still needed to build to replace the rotted one he'd ripped off, leaving the cement steps as the only access to the front door. "I'll get to it," he snapped, thinking he'd just broil the steaks in the oven instead.

Candy raised an eyebrow, and of course he didn't miss the note of disapproval in her expression. He wondered whether she was about to say something else or remind him again that he needed to finish what he'd started. The problem was that Neil was an idea man. He excelled at planning, organizing, and having others implement and build.

Candy lifted her hands, maybe in surrender, and started back up the steps and into the bathroom. Neil followed, carrying his son. The large bathroom had a nice round tub and a separate glassed-in shower. There were also a washer and dryer and double sinks. It was a bright room done in pale green and gold. Candy was running the water in the tub, and Cat was already pulling off her wet mud-soaked clothes, reaching behind her ear, taking off the cochlear implant fastened there and handing it to Neil before climbing into the bath. She looked up again to Neil as she sat and signed that the water was warm. Neil undressed Michael and lifted him in the bath with his sister, pulling out the bath toys from under the sink and piling them in as Candy turned off the water after the tub had filled. She was still sitting on the floor, her arm on the side, when she looked over her shoulder and up to him. Maybe she thought he would have left, or maybe she was trying to figure out what to say to him—he wasn't sure which. Right now, he wanted her to say something, anything, that would help cut through the distance he still felt between them.

"We should probably talk about this later. The kids…" she started, but Neil was already shaking his head.

"Cat can't hear anything, and Michael's too young, that is, unless you're planning on fighting, and I have no intention of doing that in front of them. I just want to know why. Why wouldn't you tell me, Candy?"

This time, she didn't look away. Maybe she'd had time to think about what to say or come to some conclusion about how to address this. "It wasn't my secret to share, Neil." She held up her hand as if she knew he was about to challenge her and deny and argue, which he was. It was just who he was, all those alpha tendencies that made him want to control everything, but he stopped and stared at her hand instead of pushing, as he once would have. That was, he reminded himself again, what had almost ended his marriage. He shuffled his stance and looked down as if he needed to ground himself again.

"How can you say that, really? Candy, this is you and me, our marriage, us together, and that secret was the kind of thing you shouldn't have kept from me. It was the kind of thing we need to share." He was trying to reason with her, to get her to understand, because the last thing he wanted was them harboring this kind of thing, which was a pretty big something, from each other.

"I understand that, Neil, and I agree with you for the most part, but the circumstances weren't so black and white. You must understand why your dad did it, why he told me?"

He was crossing his arms now, digging in, wondering how she could justify any of it. If she said one more time that it was complicated, he realized he'd have to step out of the bathroom, because his children would start to pick up that Mom and Dad were fighting, and that was the one thing he didn't ever want his children to experience.

"Neil, I can see how much this bothers you, and for the most part I understand why you'd be upset. I tried to tell your parents, I explained and reasoned with your mom, too, that you'd understand…" She stopped talking, maybe because he was shaking his head, feeling his stubbornness really dig in. "Oh, I see," she said, and her expression took on a sympathy that made him feel like crap—and furious. "You don't understand. Wow, Neil, I guess your mom was right."

CHAPTER 5

Candy was dressed in a sleeveless white tank with a turtleneck collar. She pulled on gold hoops and brushed her long dark hair until it shone. She added just a hint of blush and mascara only. She didn't need much in the way of makeup, and this was just family coming for dinner. She'd pulled on a pair of black capris and slipped her feet into gold sandals. She knew she was pushing it with the weather, dressing more for a warmer climate than the cool and chilly springtime in the Pacific Northwest, but the fact was that she found herself missing the heat, the warmth, the sun, and the white sandy beach. It was something that had been in her blood, a place she'd never considered moving from until Cat had come along, and then Michael.

Now here she was, living close to Emily and Brad, which really tipped the scale in her decision. Emily was her best friend, and Brad would always be her confidant, her friend, the big brother she'd never had. He had been there for her when Maria, the surrogate, had tried to turn her life upside down, when her husband had lied to her, and that had been the first time she'd understood what it meant to be part of a family. No matter what happened to her and Neil, Brad and Emily would always be there for her, no questions asked. That meant more than anything, and it removed her one aching fear: the fear of being alone. Brad and Emily would never allow her to be alone.

She clambered down the stairs, her sandals clipping softly on the carpet as she listened to Michael babbling and Cat talking in her flat voice to Neil, who was in the kitchen, putting the finishing touches on dinner. Yes, Neil, her husband, who was still trying to find his footing after putting his resort up for sale and walking away from his million-dollar deals for a quiet, simple life in this small corner of the world, was in fact a damn good cook. As with everything Neil did, there was nothing plain, simple, or ordinary about the meals he made. There were vegetables—carrots, beets, broccoli, and squash on a roasting pan tossed with oil, seasonings, and some fresh herbs. She could smell the savory aroma before she walked into the kitchen. There were also stuffed potatoes, what looked like the fixings for a gourmet salad, and the food processor out for a homemade dressing in the making. She loved his salad dressings.

The oven dinged, and Neil opened the gas range, lifting out a white cake. When had he had time to whip that up? She took a whiff, and of course her mouth watered as she took in the smells from this gourmet feast.

"You made a cake?" She looked at her husband, who had showered and changed into another T-shirt. This one was a Seahawks shirt, which was unusual, since Neil had never been one for sports T-shirts—another change to his persona. She half expected him to have on a dress shirt and khakis, but no. He also had on another pair of jeans and was barefoot with a bib apron over his shirt. It too was a look that was freaking sexy. Did the man have no idea what he was doing to her?

"Of course," he said, setting it on a cooling rack and then pulling open the fridge to lift out a bowl of strawberries and a carton of whipped cream. "Just a simple butter cake, but the kids will love it. What's a dinner without a fantastic dessert to go along with it?"

"Oh, my waistline," she said, taking in the food. Her children seemed to love being in the kitchen with Daddy. Michael had the pots cupboard open and was pulling out everything so he could climb in. Neil didn't seem to mind in the least. Cat was at the table, coloring.

Neil leaned down and kissed Candy on her cheek. "Your waistline looks just fine to me. Can you grab the napkins and plates and set the dining room table? I have a bottle of white in the fridge chilling. Thought you might like a glass. It's the sauvignon blanc from the local winery I know you love."

That was another one of the things she truly loved about Neil, that he always knew what she loved, and everything he did was for her. He may have been controlling, arrogant, and pushy at times, but there was one thing Neil could never be faulted for: He was considerate and always remembered what she liked. He went out of his way to make sure she and the children always came first. She loved him for that.

Candy didn't move as she glanced over at their oversized steel fridge, watching Neil as he lifted his own glass of red and took a swallow before smiling down at Michael over the mess he was making, then over to Cat, their beautiful girl who was so happy.

"What?" he said. She didn't realize he'd also been watching her, her amazing man who could handle everything and make it look so easy.

"Neil, I hope you don't think badly of your parents or your mom. I have to say this." She glanced over to Cat and then lowered her voice. Her husband could change in an instant from being outgoing to closed off and annoyed. He was shaking his head, and she could tell he was struggling with what to say to her. "I'm not sure what I can say, Neil. What's going through that head of yours? Maybe you need to tell me what you know, because all I can think of is that maybe you don't know everything. If you did, I think you'd be a little understanding." She said it softly, hoping she was getting through to him, but Neil, being Neil, could be far from giving, understanding, and considerate at times, especially when he seemed to have his mind made up about something—which appeared to be the case now.

"What can I say, Candy? My mom cheated with, of all people, God forbid, my uncle, that dog, a man who's the worst of the worst in leading women astray. How could she have picked him?" His voice was anything but friendly as he set his glass down and opened the oven again, this time to put in the vegetables.

He put his hand on Candy's arm and led her from the kitchen, still keeping the kids in view. She didn't step away but rested her hand on Neil's chest, looking up at the hurt that lingered.

"How did you find out?" she asked, and this time he couldn't hide whatever it was in his expression that haunted him.

"My uncle, of all people. It was after the funeral. Brad, me, Jed, and Andy were there. Dad, too. It was a bad scene. Uncle Todd was angry, lashing out, and it was Dad he was trying to hurt. He let enough slip that we knew something had happened with Mom. It was enough that Dad had no choice but to tell us that night, the whole story of what happened. I still can't believe it, and you know it was hard to listen. Everything I believed about my parents and their rock solidness crumbled in my mind. Everything I grew up believing was a lie. I didn't know what to say, but it hurt more than anything that Dad said he'd shared it with you." Neil was looking right at her with something that seemed so accusing—so hurt.

She firmed her lips, trying to decide what to say, how to handle something so delicate and help her husband get over his disillusionment. "You should know something, Neil. What your parents shared, all that pain and hurt and ugliness…your dad opening his heart to me, that was the turning point for us."

He seemed curious about that, as his expression told her he was really studying her.

"It was your mom and dad, their story, Neil, that happened so long ago, listening to them and hitting rock bottom…it made me give you another chance. Your dad knew I was leaving even though I hadn't decided myself, but you'd lied to me, hurt me, and your parents understood better than anyone that hurt, the betrayal, the lies, the deception." She poked his chest. "So don't you dare be too hard on your mom or your dad, because to me they're heroes. They didn't make an excuse for what happened. They shared something so deeply personal to them with me because they knew our story was heading down that slippery slope and could so easily have become theirs."

She could hear a truck pull in and didn't need to turn to the window or race to the door to know that Brad, Emily, and the kids were there. She patted Neil's chest and stepped in closer, reaching up as she pressed a kiss to Neil's full, soft lips and took in the shock, passion, and fire that made Neil who he was, the difficult man he could be.

"Now let's have a nice visit, and if you still need to

hash this out, then we'll talk later," she said, then rubbed his chest and stepped back.

He gave her an odd look as if she'd just turned the tables on him. Then he let out a harsh laugh before reaching for her and pulling her back in his arms and leaning in. His warm breath fluttered over her lips as he kissed her again, this time letting her know exactly what she meant to him.

CHAPTER 6

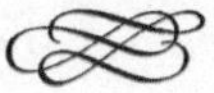

I t was the laughter he loved, sitting around the table after downing a bottle of wine, with food, conversation, family, and good times. Neil went to fill Brad's glass, but he shook his head and covered it. "No more for this boy. I'm driving. Great meal, though. Impressed you threw all this together, brother dear. Maybe you should look at opening a restaurant."

He couldn't believe Brad had suggested that. Even though Neil was beginning to notice the number of times Brad had hinted at what he should do with the rest of his life, he hadn't come right out and said anything so blunt and to the point yet. Neil was starting to notice the way Brad's gaze had landed on all the projects he'd started in the house, which he still hadn't finished. He knew his brother well and knew the hinting would soon give way to questioning, asking, telling, and ultimatums.

Neil, though, wasn't ready to answer Brad and hoped he'd drop it, but he'd been doing that for months.

"So what are you going to do, Neil?" Brad tapped the

table with his fingers. "Have you figured out yet what it is that's really important, what it is you're going to do with the rest of your life?"

Okay, so Brad was way past the dropping-hints stage; he was jumping right to putting Neil on the spot. He was also giving him a glare that said he wouldn't back down, a look he gave his kids whenever they mouthed off to Emily and he was forced to lay down the law. *Of course, leave it to Brad,* Neil thought as he gazed at his brother across the table, *to bring up the elephant in the room.* Neil had always been able to think on his feet and come up with something, anything, but for the first time in his life he couldn't come up with one reasonable thing to say, so he leaned back in his chair, taking in Candy beside him with her hands flat on the table beside her plate, which held a piece of steak pushed to the side that she hadn't finished. She wore his rock on her finger, a square pink diamond surrounded by more diamonds. It could keep them in comfort for a while. Why were his thoughts continuing to go down that road?

He could see Emily touch Brad and give him a look that said he shouldn't have pushed, but no one was saying anything. It was now quiet, so quiet all he could hear was the tick of the clock. The tension escalated, as everyone seemed to be waiting for him to say something, anything to break this icy silence. The kids, thankfully, were playing in the other room, leaving the adults alone in the dining room to drink some wine and catch up. He wished for a moment that one of them would come in and break up this standoff.

"Honestly, Brad, I don't have a clue." He glanced over to his big brother, who was watching him as if he felt his role was to take Neil by the collar and lead him. He didn't like it, and he resented the way it was making him feel, but Brad, being Brad, wouldn't let it go.

He gestured at Neil. "Look at you. I'm seriously starting to get a little worried. First it's the hair, then the beard, and now an earring. What's going on with you, Neil?" Brad said, sounding a *lot* worried, talking to him as if he were sixteen years old. Even Emily was watching him as if someone needed to do something. He wasn't sure whether he'd growled or if it was all in his head.

"Look, would everyone please stop? We're good, okay? I'm awesome. Just need to figure out what I can make work here, is all. I have some things in the works, just not willing to talk about them yet." He had jack shit in the works, but his brother didn't need to know that—or the fact that he didn't have a dime left in his bank account. The electricity bill had just come, and he couldn't for the life of him figure out where he was going to get the money from next. It was the first time he'd had to consider dialing it back on their spending, figuring out quick what he could sell, or restructuring to get some funds back in his name.

"Well, why don't we talk it out? I'm here. Let's discuss some options, bounce them off me, because you've been back for a few months, and I don't see much happening except stuff piling up for you to do, some new ideas, but you haven't followed through with anything."

"Brad." Emily rubbed his arm. Her voice was laced with warning, but Brad was now shaking his head with that stubbornness he got when he somehow figured out that he needed to fix things himself. Neil didn't need fixing, though. He was just having trouble figuring out what he could do.

He realized Candy was awfully quiet beside him, and he didn't miss her shared glance with Brad, the way she worried her lower lip between her teeth. Something was going on there.

"Neil, I asked Brad to talk to you," she said in a low

voice. For the second time today, he was feeling as if his wife was confiding elsewhere, with his brother, when she should have been with him. He turned and looked down at Candy and the guilty expression on her face. "I'm sorry, but I've been patient, watching and waiting and…" She stopped talking, and he had a bad feeling he wasn't going to like what she was going to say next.

"What, is this like an intervention?" He was about ready to toss his napkin on the table, push back his chair, and leave when Candy reached over and grabbed his wrist.

"Neil, wait." She paused and slid around, taking a breath as if considering what to say. To him, it seemed they were getting farther apart instead of closing the distance between them.

"Tell him, Candy," Brad said, and Neil realized his wife was looking to Brad for more and more. That was something he wasn't about to stand for.

She cleared her throat. "Neil, I was at the store yesterday and went to use your credit card to buy a new pair of boots for Cat. You know her old ones have holes, and water's been leaking in…and your credit card was declined, both of them." Her cheeks reddened in embarrassment.

Shit, he was mortified. He hadn't realized she was using them. He should have said something, made some excuse to take them back. No one said a word, and all Neil could do was lean back and run his hand over his beard as he tried to digest his humiliation and betrayal at the fact that his wife hadn't told him. "You felt you needed to go and run to my brother and tell him, that you couldn't tell me?" he said. "Now who's keeping secrets, Candy?"

Maybe it was the way he was staring at her, as if she'd just turned her back on him, that made her slip back her chair and excuse herself from the dining room. Neil took in his brother across the table, whose expression said he was fast losing his patience.

"Neil, your wife wouldn't have said a word to me, so stop being a prick. The fact was that I was there. I ran into her at the feed store where she was in line in front of me. She was humiliated when the clerk told her loud enough that everyone could hear. She pulled out a second card, and it was declined, too, so I paid for the boots. She didn't have to say anything for me to know that you've gotten yourself into another financial jam and have been hiding it from her."

Now he felt like crap. He watched as Emily excused herself, her lips tight, her face flushed as she scooted back her chair and slipped out of the room, maybe to see where Candy had gone off to. Her face said it all: She was embarrassed for him, as well.

Neil didn't know what to say as he rested his elbows on the table. He couldn't think of a time he'd ever been in this kind of hole, feeling as if everything was caving in around him. Brad wasn't making it easy. He just sat there, watching and waiting him out. "I'm stuck, Brad. The resort hasn't sold, and when we all chipped in for Andy, that took pretty much all I had left. There's nothing coming in, and everything is going out."

This was a part of life he'd never experienced. He'd always had enough money before. He was the one who always offered, who helped out.

"What can I do to help?" Brad leaned forward, his voice low so the women didn't hear, looking at Neil so intently. It was that big-brotherly look he was taking on more and more with all of them. He had the broadest shoulders of them all, Neil could see it, and he wondered, when would it become too much? After all, everyone had a breaking point.

"I don't know, honestly. I've never been in a position like this before. I always knew my place in a more fast-moving world, where deals were made with wining and dining, traveling with high-class folks—a world that makes my wife uncomfortable." He didn't want to say any more, because he'd been telling himself over and over that it didn't matter, that he just needed to shift his way of thinking to something smaller, more low key, something that would make Candy happy.

"We were all worried about you, Neil, wondering how you were going to be happy here in this quiet small community when you had that world-class resort and the ranching business with Dad down in Cancun. You had your hand in how many other investments? It was always something, and to you it was just what you did before breakfast. Not my world, but we knew you were happy." Brad just watched him, and Neil realized he couldn't stay quiet anymore.

"I don't think I can do this here. I need something more that excites me. I just don't know how to have the lifestyle, the business, and my family." He sighed, leaning back as if he'd denied what he was feeling for too long. It felt good to say it out loud.

He heard someone clear her throat, and he didn't have to turn to know it was his wife standing there in the doorway, Emily with her, holding a tray of mugs while Candy carried a pot of coffee.

"Then what is it you need, Neil?" she said. "Because right now it seems we don't have a lot of choices anymore. You need to figure out what you're going to do, what we're going to do." Candy set the pot on the table, but she didn't sit down beside Neil. Instead, she looked over to Brad and then back to him. Before she could say a word, Neil lifted his hand as the idea hit him.

"You're right. What I need to do is come up with a business plan."

CHAPTER 7

After saying goodnight to Brad, Emily, and the kids and tucking Cat and Michael into bed for the night, Candy strode into their bedroom, hearing the crackle of wood in the open fireplace. Neil had lit the fire, and she loved listening to the sounds and the peace it created in their bedroom as she sat there with him, in his arms, mesmerized by the flames. It was the perfect romantic setting, and Neil was a master at creating romance of any kind. She wished sometimes she had his skills and confidence, but the man had seen and experienced many aspects of life Candy had never been comfortable with.

She took in her husband, who was sitting in the light blue stuffed easy chair, his feet up on the ottoman. She half expected to see him with another glass of wine, as she also realized he'd been drinking more and more of late. It wasn't uncommon for him to have two, three glasses of wine a night. She frowned at that thought, worrying for a minute, since her father had lived as a drunk and died drunk. It wasn't that Neil was an alcoholic, just that he was turning to something that could be a problem. Maybe it was time to say something.

He was running his hand over the short beard he'd started. It was dark and made his full lips seem a darker red than they were. She strode over to him slowly and stopped at the stool as he lifted his feet so she could sit on the ottoman. He rested his bare feet on her lap, and it was instinct to start rubbing and massaging. He shut his eyes as if her touch pleased him and leaned back, breathing deeply.

"So what happened to the buyer who was considering the resort? Why is he still on the fence?" Maybe she should have asked more of the details before now.

Neil, though, didn't open his eyes as he said, "I've been starting to wonder the same thing. It's been how many months of him going through the day-to-day operations to see whether everything fits with his chain? I'm beginning to think the man's stringing me along." Neil opened his eyes, and she could tell by how the light amber flickered a little darker that he was now having concerns she hadn't seen before. "Just one more thing I've let slip," he said. "I don't honestly know, and if Andy and Brad knew, or even Jed, how lax I've been with my business, I think they'd serve my head up on a platter."

He sighed, but she understood what he was saying. Neil had once been shrewd, smart, sharp, not missing anything. Maybe some of this was her fault.

"I haven't pushed," he said. "I should have, but…" He stopped and sighed and reached for her hand, pulling it closer. "I haven't been keeping things from you, if that's what you're going to ask." He squeezed her hand. "Except the money. Sorry, I should have said something. I can only imagine how embarrassed you were. It was on my mind to tell you not to use the credit cards."

"It's not the money, Neil. You know how uneasy I am about all the money you had. I've always had a simple life. I know what it means to struggle to just get by. It's just that you should have told me it was as bad as it is. Didn't your dad buy you out, your share of the Cancun ranch, the estate? You were going to sell it all to him, I thought, or did you already, and that money is gone, too?" She pulled her hand away and rested them both on his feet. Of course, she was conflicted with these secrets, wondering what they'd both driven each other to.

He was shaking his head. "I never finished anything. Started to, and then when we left Cancun and came back home, I just…" He was at a loss. She could tell by the way he patted the arm of the chair.

She'd never seen Neil like this, as if he'd lost his footing, and she couldn't help worrying that she was somehow responsible for part of it. After all, she was the one who'd wanted a simple life. He'd done all this for her.

"Don't do that, Candy," he said, watching her. "I can tell what you're thinking. This isn't all on you. This is me, what I've done. I messed up so many things because of my obsession that I'm still backpedaling through the cleanup. Let me be clear. I screwed up. I gave Maria five million to go away, and it left me with very little. Yes, if Dad buys my share out, we'll be okay, but I haven't pushed there. I mentioned it once, but Dad told me to think about it some more. Not sure why. Maybe he thinks I just need time to reconsider and figure everything out. The resort…selling that would set us up quite comfortably for life, and I'd have something to start something new, but for the life of me, I haven't got a clue what that would be."

He ran his hand over his longish hair, the waves curling at the ends, hiding his ears. It was a look that was so different from the clean-cut Neil she'd fallen in love with.

"Something happened, too, when we went to Jed and Diana's. Seems Andy's mother isn't beyond reaching from the grave. She'd planned before she died to get rid of Laura and was hiring someone to plan an accident." He sighed, and she felt her stomach bottom out. She wondered whether her alarm showed on her face.

She'd never seen this expression in her husband's eyes, and he reached for her, pulling her onto his lap and holding her close to him. She could feel how tense he was, and, as he was holding her now, she could also feel his need to keep her a little closer. At the same time, she was reeling from hearing something so awful. She didn't know much about Andy's parents, only that his mother was from a wealthy eastern blueblood family, and his father had stashed a herd of mistresses. Andy had once terrified her with his dark, brooding ways, but now she couldn't help admiring the man because of all he'd walked away from to keep his family safe.

"You said 'planned,' but is she going to be all right?" Her voice squeaked. "That's horrible, Neil. What did you all do?" She sat up and looked down on him. His jaw was tight, and she could tell he was really bothered.

"We met with the person, we found out…" He shut his eyes, shaking his head. "Let's just say the person who was arranging it made sure it didn't happen. Caroline's gone now, and any threat to Laura's gone, as well. We ended up paying this person her price for not doing the job. How sick is that? So between Jed, Brad, Andy, and me, we shared her asking price, and I had to pull the money from everywhere I could, and it left us with nothing. I'm sorry."

She didn't know what to say. She wondered by the sheepish look he'd given her whether he thought she was angry with him for what he did, but she said, "I'm glad you did that."

Maybe it was surprise that flickered in his gaze. "Really, you're not mad?"

She shook her head. "Only that you didn't say anything, but you are now. I'm just glad Laura will be safe. It's not a question. Of course you should have paid. You have no idea how it makes me feel that you and your brothers, and Andy, too, would come together and help each other out."

"I would give it all for you. So would my brothers, and Andy. We'd never hesitate to give everything up for you, for our women." He reached up and touched her face so gently. There was so much love there as she leaned in to his touch.

"And that's why I think you need to consider a new plan." She touched his chest, smoothing her hand over the blue lettering of his shirt.

"Oh, and what would this be?"

"Your business plan. I think you need to start back at the beginning and take your resort back."

"Candy." He was shaking his head. His expression said enough to her that she knew he was thinking of all the reasons why that wasn't a good idea. "I promised you, and you're more important than the resort, than all of it."

"Hey, I know that, which is why you need to take it back. It's a part of who you are and what makes up Neil Friessen, my husband and the man I fell in love with. You need to go in and say to the buyers that they had their chance, but the deal's off the table. It's still in your name, right? So reclaim what's yours, go and make it bigger, better, and be the king-of-the-world business owner I know you can be. It's what you're good at. It's your world, and you shine in it. You, here…" She took in the bedroom she loved and this small corner of the Pacific Northwest where she loved living. It was peaceful, quiet, but her husband was slowly dying inside. "You're trying to change who you are, to make a square peg fit into a round hole. It doesn't work, Neil. It's not working. You're becoming miserable."

"Candy, I don't want to do anything that's going to make you uncomfortable. Fitting into that world is something you aren't comfortable with, and I love you and the kids more than having that, being all of that. As happy as I was, there was a huge part of me that was so lonely, and that's the part only you can fill."

"Hey, who said anything about me not being there with you? We'll make it work. You'll make it work," she said. At the same time, an unsettled feeling she hadn't felt in a long time squeezed her chest, giving a little hiccup in her breath as she pulled another in, but she ignored it. Was she suggesting the one thing that could end up tearing them apart?

CHAPTER 8

Neil loved nothing more than making love with his wife, and he didn't quite know what had come over him as he stirred from sleep with his wife under him, her legs around his waist. He pinned her hands above her head and drove himself deeper into her. He was moving fast and then slow, changing his rhythm to drive hard and deep as he held her where she was. She was making soft noises and whimpering, and he could tell how close she was to going over the edge, tossing her head side to side and then tightening around him, but he didn't stop. He kept going, pushing her, moving inside her in a way that left her completely at his mercy until he felt himself coming apart and burying himself completely inside her. She cried out under him, and he allowed himself to let go.

He wondered whether he'd fallen asleep, passed out on top of her, as he felt Candy's hand slide up and down his back lightly, tracing small circles over and over. He was still inside her, where he loved to be, but he couldn't explain this change in him. He couldn't have enough of her tonight. She was amazing, his wife, sexy as all hell. She said nothing as she lay there quietly with him, just staying in the moment.

He finally lifted his head and glanced down at her quiet beauty, her dark toffee-colored eyes, her silky long dark hair spread over the pillow, and her lips, which he loved to sample over and over. He pressed a tender kiss there, holding it for a moment before pulling out and moving beside her, lying on his side so he could look over at her, nose to nose, so close he could touch her lips with his. She just watched him, not saying a word. This was the love and passion that burned inside her for him, which she couldn't hide.

"Was I too rough?" He touched her face with the back of his hand as if he needed to hold on to her. He wondered at times where her head went, what she was thinking, and he found himself remembering the journal on the writing desk in the corner of their bedroom, its dark blue cover. She left it sitting there all day, every day, and not once had he opened it.

She just stared at him as a slow smile touched her lips. It was subtle, and he waited until it lit up her eyes. Then he knew she was okay.

"No, but wow. What got into you? You were insatiable last night. I love making love with you, but you haven't seemed too interested as of late."

Did she have any idea what she did to him? Maybe it was because of this feeling he'd had for so long that he wasn't good enough for her. "I don't know," he said. "It felt as if you gave something back to me. Can't explain it."

She didn't say anything, but the way she watched him again was as if she knew. She rolled on her side, the sheet falling away, showing off her magnificent breasts—the full creaminess and roundness he loved to explore, to touch, to taste. She was nose to nose, sharing his pillow as she stared at him and then reached for his hand, holding it. "I'm glad. I wasn't sure what I could do for you, but I'm happy to have you back."

The way she said it, he started to wonder about a lot of things, his moodiness and brooding and floundering. Neil was all about business, always had been. "I can't explain it, but you know that excitement you have when you're doing something you love, something that excites you, stirs your blood, and fills you with such joy? When you gave me the idea last night, I just couldn't stop it from flowing." He threw back the covers and slipped out of bed naked, watching the easy smile that lit up his wife's face as she watched him stride around. Her hands were tucked under her cheek as she lay curled up on her side. The way she watched him made him feel so good. This was the first time she didn't have that deer-in-the-headlights look at any mention of his resort, his million-dollar deals, or being part of something with him that was way out of her comfort zone. Maybe she was ready.

"You know," he said, "it would be fantastic first if we could fly back to Cancun, meet with the builder. There was a financier I was considering partnering with to expand the resort to be part of a worldwide diamond chain." He was on a roll, and it took him a second to realize Candy had looked away and was now sitting up. Their king-size bed with its intricate post design was the centerpiece of the room, except for the fact that his wife, sitting in the middle of that magnificent bed, appeared to be unsettled now. The change was enough to make him sift through his head. He'd been thinking out loud about his plans and how excited he was, but maybe something had spooked her.

"Whoa, seriously, Candy, what did I just do?" He was worried as he smoothed back his hair, his hands resting on the side of his head now. She was pulling away.

She gave her head a shake, pasted a smile to her face, and hesitated only a second before slipping out of bed and walking toward him with her gorgeous, sexy body. The scar that had left her unable to have children had faded now. She touched him, and there was a mist in her eyes as she looked up at him. "I just never realized how much I was holding you back—and for that I'm truly sorry."

CHAPTER 9

She pressed her hand to her chest over the soft satin of her lavender housecoat, wondering whether the shock on her face resembled the jolt that was zinging through her as she took in her husband and his cleanly shaven face. He was dressed in dark dress pants, a leather belt, and a navy dress shirt. The only thing missing was a tie. He smiled as he walked right up to her and kissed her open mouth, as she'd been gawking. Her hand slid up to her throat before falling to her side.

"I can see you're a little taken aback." He was standing over her, looking down, and he winked in that flirty way of his that she hadn't seen in a long time.

No, the Neil she'd seen over the past year was one who had taken to growing his hair, refusing to shave, and dressing casually as if he'd decided to check himself out on a permanent vacation.

"You like?" he said. He'd even thrown on that cologne she loved, which wasn't overpowering but had her wanting to run her hands over his face and then link them around his neck, reaching up and breathing in the clean, spicy, intoxicating scent that had always rattled her.

"Don't know what to say, Neil," she said. What she did do was giggle as she touched her mouth, hearing Michael and Cat behind her clatter at the table, eating cereal and calling out for Daddy. Of course, Neil bent over and kissed each of them until they were laughing. She wondered for a moment whether he'd be upset with their dirty hands on his clean shirt. She couldn't remember a time he'd been around them dressed so…nice.

He pulled away before they could run milk-soaked hands over him. "I have a meeting with my banker to go plead for money, and then I have some ideas I wanted to talk to you about."

She couldn't remember him ever including her like he was, and for a moment she realized one of the concerns she'd had was that he'd drift back to the old Neil, who just went ahead and steamrolled over her, leaving her without a clue as to what was going on.

He ran his thumb over the crease above her nose, between her eyebrows. "Hey, I promised you before that I'd never keep you in the dark again. I'm just sifting some ideas around and want to make sure you're on board before we do anything." He leaned in and kissed her again.

"Well, what about the banker?" she asked, and he sighed.

"For one, we need a line of credit to keep going so I can keep the bills paid until I get a viable business income coming in. I shouldn't have drained us like I did, but…"

"You weren't thinking clearly, but helping Andy is what you should have done. I can't fault you for that."

He had a way of giving all of himself to her that he'd never had before. It was in a look, a touch, or saying nothing at all. "I love you. You know that, right?" he said again with a flicker of worry.

"I know. That's been the one thing I've never questioned." She reached up and slipped her hand over the smooth skin of his cheek. "I'm going to miss my rough-around-the-edges Neil, but I do like this one, too. So I need to ask before you go: Do any of the ideas have us going back to Cancun, back to the estate, living back with your mom and dad?"

All the happiness he'd had moments before changed to something resembling disillusionment.

"Oh, Neil, this thing with your mom…why can't you see it the way I do?"

He made a sound of frustration as he stepped away, becoming distracted, letting her know he didn't want to consider her side, but she really looked at him, waiting him out until he glanced back at her.

"I don't know, Candy. I bought this house, this place here for us. I still own the estate with Dad. I can't see it your way, I'm sorry. This is my mom, who I had an image of in my head for so long. She and Dad were perfect. They were my inspiration for a family, all that dedication and love, and to find out they were just like everyone else, flawed, not the picture-perfect parents I believed they were…I'm having a hard time coming to terms with any of it, let alone understanding it. Us, this family…" He gestured with enough force that she knew he was digging in, standing his ground. "We're not cheaters. That was pounded into us by my parents, by my dad, only for me to learn that my mom is a hypocrite."

She was taken aback by the venom and judgement. She didn't know what to say to get him to understand that it wasn't all that cut and dried. Everything wasn't always that simple. Maybe that was what this came down to—that her husband, who'd controlled everything about their relationship and his business until he'd nearly destroyed them, was losing control.

"Neil, you're so wrong. If you recall, what you did with Maria was cheating, in a way, much like what your dad did with that neighbor woman, giving his attention to her, spending time with her."

His eyes flashed with an anger she hadn't seen in a long time. "And you're like my mom, with that doctor who befriended you in Cancun. How much more would it have taken before he had you in his bed? Is that what you're saying?"

His words were like a slap in the face. Maybe he realized he'd gone too far, as he stepped away, reached for his keys, and left.

CHAPTER 10

She lifted the dirt with the blade of the shovel and then pulled out the weeds to dump them into the wheelbarrow at the edge of the driveway. She really loved their landscaping, with mature yellow and pink rosebushes, a peach tree, a wisteria, and small bushes she didn't know the name of. They'd become overgrown in such a short time, and with the new buds of spring starting, this was the time to cut them back. She was drawn into the colors, wondering what else she could plant in front. She'd love to pick up some marigolds, impatiens, asters, daisies. She loved daisies. Then there were all the colors of annuals. They were so impractical, and she'd never really lived in a place that could have any—nor had she had the money to toss away on them. Then, they didn't anymore, as she'd just found out.

She couldn't help thinking of Neil's mom and her spectacular gardens. She'd loved the fragrant tropical flowers down in Cancun. It was a stunning place, the estate, but it was a place that had never been hers and never could be.

This was the first place that was just theirs, hers and

Neil's, where she could create something that belonged to just them, making changes, adding, enhancing. She couldn't have done that at the estate down south. She jammed the shovel in the dirt, glancing over again at Michael, who had his own plastic shovel, digging up the dirt in a planter. He was making a mess but having such fun. Cat was on the bicycle Neil had bought her with training wheels, riding around on the front driveway. She was wearing her pink helmet with ladybugs.

She heard the gate open, and for a minute she blinked, wondering who was there, as Neil had only been gone about half an hour, if that. She watched the dark truck pull in, Brad's truck, and she only had a moment to wonder who was behind the wheel when she spotted Brad, who honked, maybe to catch Cat's attention. She put her foot down and stopped, pulling over to the side, looking up, straddling her bike with both sneakered feet on the ground.

"Hi, there." Brad came around the truck and touched the top of Cat's helmet. Leaning down, he said something to her that Candy couldn't make out, but Cat was smiling up at her uncle before she started to pedal again.

Brad was still smiling as he glanced her way, dressed as he always was, in blue jeans, a blue checked shirt with the sleeves rolled up, and his belt with a silver buckle. As always, he looked so good, and he appeared to take in everything and everyone in that moment—a guy who took care of everything. "Neil here?" he asked, stepping closer, taking in the goofy grin on Michael's face as he held on to the large ceramic pot, digging in the dirt and tossing it on the ground.

"No, he went out to the bank," Candy said, leaning on her shovel, reaching up and wiping back the strand of hair that had come loose from the messy bun she'd pinned her long hair up in.

"Everything okay?" He stepped closer, looking at her with the big-brother look he'd mastered. Then, he'd always been someone for Candy to lean on. Even though he was Neil's brother, she knew he would never take sides. He'd be there for her, as well. It meant more to her than she could explain to anyone, but it bothered Neil, too.

She shrugged. "We kind of had a fight." Why had she needed to say something?

Brad crossed his arms, looking down at her. "Do you want to talk about it?"

She smiled over at her brother-in-law. At times, she envied Emily for having a man like Brad, but they were so suited for each other. She took in how broad his shoulders were. He was the one everyone leaned on, though they all came together to help one another out. Brad was different, however. He was the one who seemed to keep the family together with his role of big brother. They looked up to him. Candy looked up to him, though she loved Neil deeply.

"Neil shaved off that beard he started, came down dressed for business. I was starting to wonder where the old Neil had disappeared to. He doesn't want to walk away from the resort, the business. I know he agreed to for me, for us to have a new start, but it wasn't entirely fair for me to think he could be happy up here, living a simple life. He's not happy, as you can tell. He's going through the motions."

Brad gave her an odd look she wasn't sure she understood.

She shrugged. "Neil isn't made the same as you and Jed. Even Andy is more settled. Neil needs more. I just hadn't realized how much."

"Neil always was the one with the ideas, and by the time any of us had a chance to think about something,

Neil was already off implementing it." Brad was shaking his head. "He would line up backers and have everyone in place to start the work while the rest of us were still standing there, feeling at times as if he'd just yanked the rug out from under us. He was the idea guy, never one to get his hands dirty—other than working with wood. He played around with carpentry for a while. It was always something that inspired him, but not enough, I guess. He starts things, as you can see, and he does pitch in, but physical labor doesn't drive him as it does me, Jed, and Dad. Even Andy is happy getting his hands dirty and finishing what he's started. Neil's the one who always wanted to own the world, to look for something bigger," Brad said, and Candy had to agree. "But what about you, Candy? This can't all be about Neil. I thought you didn't want Cancun, the resort, that life?"

She had to look up at the concern in his expression.

"Neil loves being the center of attention, always has," Brad said. "He's comfortable and thrives in the wheelin' and dealin' life. I remember a time it scared the hell out of you. Do you think you could go back with Neil and be part of that?"

It really was a great question, but the fact was she knew she couldn't, even considering it was something Neil did all the time. That kind of thing would have Candy slowly going out of her mind. She liked the quiet, her family, her home, and her horse and donkey. She didn't know how to schmooze the kinds of people Neil needed to be in business with, and she didn't want to learn. Her stomach ached thinking about it. "I think you already know the answer to that, but I can't ask Neil to give everything up for me and be miserable."

"So what are you going to do?" he said, watching her.

She wished he'd offer some words of wisdom,

because right now she didn't see a happy outcome for either her or Neil. "I don't know, Brad. I don't want to see Neil unhappy or disillusioned as he is now. He came alive last night for the first time since I could remember, excited in a way he hasn't been in a long time. I can't take that from him. I can't ask him again to give it up. He's not happy, even though he told me he could be. Look at everything." She gestured to the yard, the house. "He gets an idea, spends a pile of money, and never finishes anything—the deck, the patio... The barbecue is still boxed, and now he's talking about building Cat an outdoor play center. The money he's tossing away is money we don't have."

Brad was nodding, looking down at Michael, who was now shoving a handful of dirt in his mouth. "Michael, don't eat that!" Brad said, laughing as he reached down and wiped the dirt off Michael's tongue before lifting him in his arms. "Do you want me to talk to Neil?" he asked. "I could sit him down and help him get his head on straight."

"I would, but I think I need to work this out with him. What I would prefer is if you talked to him about your mom."

Brad appeared confused.

"Part of our fight. He told me you know what happened in your parents' past, your mom's indiscretion." For a moment, she wondered whether she should have let it go.

Brad looked away, taking a breath as if this was something he didn't want to think about, let alone talk about.

"I'm hoping you'll help Neil understand that what happened is in the past. Your mom is still your mom. He's not very happy with her, and I'm afraid your mom may be right." This time, she had Brad's attention. "Your mom told me that Neil would never understand. She never wanted any of you to know, and I know what it took from her to share it with me."

Before Brad could answer, the electronic gate opened, and Neil pulled in, driving their white SUV. When she looked up at Brad, she realized maybe he couldn't understand, either.

CHAPTER 11

Pulling in and finding his big brother speaking with his wife didn't make Neil very happy. He stepped out of his SUV and spotted Cat, who climbed off her bike and ran to him in her slow, awkward gait, stumbling just before she reached him, but Neil was ready and caught her before she could fall.

He carried her over and used that few seconds to try to dial back his irritation. He patted Cat's leg, holding her tight. "Brad, didn't know you were coming over." He didn't look over at his wife but could see that her face was flushed from awkwardness, which could have been from their fight earlier. Or maybe she was confiding in Brad again.

"Came to talk to you. Wow, you cleaned yourself up, shaved off your new look."

Candy didn't say anything as she watched Neil, an uncertainty lingering between them.

"So did my wife call you?" he asked, glancing back at Candy as she gave him a look that was pretty close to disgust and disbelief, similar to the "Drop dead" look she'd mastered for him a long time ago.

"You're such an ass sometimes, Neil," Candy said. She jabbed the shovel in the dirt, reached for Michael in Brad's arms, and gestured for Cat's hand. Neil put her down, and she walked to Candy. His wife took both kids into the house and shut the door.

"What the hell was that?" Brad gave him a look as if he'd lost his mind.

"Sorry, just on edge. I said something I shouldn't have earlier. She pushed my buttons, and I kind of lost it. Then I drive in and see you here talking to my wife."

"Hmm," Brad said, nodding and then looking toward the door. It wasn't lost on Neil that he'd said nothing to clear the air or put his worries at ease by assuring him that his wife hadn't been confiding in him again.

He really didn't want to get into anything with Brad. The fact was that he was feeling pretty shitty for how he'd talked to Candy, throwing Jim Miller, that pediatrician who'd fallen in love with her in Cancun, in her face. Comparing her to his mother had been cruel. The fact was that she was stunning, and he knew she probably had no idea of the effect she had on men. Who wouldn't want a woman like Candy? She was everything to him, and she was the only woman he'd ever wanted.

"I can see some tension here," Brad said. "Anything you want to talk about? Haven't seen you dressed up in a long time." His brother gestured to his dress shirt and pants. By the look he had, Neil wondered whether Candy had already told him where he'd been.

"You knew I was at the bank, begging. Candy told you, didn't she?"

At least this time Brad had the good graces to wince.

"Ah, so she did share that part," Neil said. Why hadn't she been able to keep that to herself? It was humiliating, having his brother look down on him, having anyone see him spiraling down, sitting at the crossroads, having lost the financial security he'd always had. Neil loved wealth. He'd always had money, had always created money, until his sound reasoning and business savvy took a backseat to his need for a child. He'd put aside his shrewdness in business and allowing his feelings to rule him, which was the one thing that separated those truly successful in business from those who weren't. That was when he'd made one of the stupidest business decisions ever: giving all his money to the surrogate so she'd leave his wife alone, leave his child alone. Now he was spiraling into a financial mess he couldn't find his way out of.

"Hey, she didn't elaborate on it. The only thing she mentioned was the resort and that you're possibly keeping it," Brad said.

"Yeah, well, that may not even be a possibility."

"Why?"

"I'm tapped right out, Brad. Never been this bad. I maxed out all credit, got nothing left to barter. The banker here got really nervous when he added up the TDS and GDS and wouldn't consider the Cancun resort as any collateral, as it's not their area of expertise." The fact was that his credit had taken a huge dip, and he was dealing with someone who didn't understand the kind of world Neil operated in. It was humiliating to sit there, ask for a simple line of credit, and then be denied. Neil Friessen had never experienced that kind of humiliation, and he had left the local bank with his tail between his legs. It was a humbling experience that he never wanted to go through again, and he'd sworn as he drove away that he'd pull everything from that branch and move it somewhere else, to a bank that appreciated and understood who Neil Friessen was.

"You paid for this house," Brad said. "What about taking out a mortgage?"

How could he tell Brad he'd taken a second one out on the house a few months before? He really did have nothing. He shook his head.

"Can I loan you something?" Brad said.

Neil couldn't even look at his brother for offering something he had no intention of taking. "I've always been the one in this family to have more. I've always been able to think fast on my feet, to swing a deal and bring in investors, but I walked away from what I was good at. Now I may have buried myself so deep in the hole that I can't get out." He was shaking his head. "No, but thank you, Brad. This is something I have to figure out myself." He started to walk away.

"Hey, Neil," Brad said, wiping his hand across his mouth as if thinking of what to say. "Maybe it's time we had a talk about Mom."

Neil just stared at Brad and then glanced over to the front door. "I wish my wife would stop confiding in you, Brad."

"Yeah, well, you need to get over yourself, because as you reminded both Jed and me, you have no intention of not being there as the self-appointed confidant for Diana and Emily, dear brother."

It wasn't funny, so why was he laughing? "Doesn't mean I'm not pissed that you come over and stick your nose into my business," Neil said, knowing he sounded like an ungrateful ass.

"Hey, I've kept my nose out of it so far, watching and waiting, but the problem is, Neil, you're drowning. You know it, I know it, and your wife knows it."

CHAPTER 12

Candy wasn't sure what had happened with Brad outside. It had gotten pretty heated, and Neil had done nothing more than step inside the house and close himself up in his office. She wasn't sure what he was doing aside from the fact that he was on his computer, making calls and leaving messages. She didn't have a clue who he was talking to.

She went and tapped on the door, then opened it without waiting for him to answer. She wondered whether he'd dismiss her, as he didn't look up right away, instead leaning back in his chair and wiping his face in a way that told her he was distracted. She didn't like this distance, so she stood there and waited.

"Kids okay?" he asked, maybe because it was always easier to ask about them than to address the problem.

"Kids are fine, Neil. I'm going to head over to Brad and Emily's and check on Sable and Ambrose." She might throw her saddle on Sable and take the hour loop. She had enough time before the sun started to go down.

Neil glanced up. "I'm kind of in the middle of something here. Can you do it tomorrow?" He didn't ask, but by the way he said it, it sounded as if it was a done deal.

"I'll take the kids with me. Katy will babysit, and you'll have a nice quiet house to yourself so you can just keep doing what you're doing." She started to back away, and Neil's expression took on an annoyance she hadn't seen in some time.

He tossed a pen he'd been holding down on the desk and pushed his chair back a little harder than he needed to. "I'm tired of you running over to my brother all the time and telling him everything. Why do you feel the need to tell him what I'm doing, what we're doing? This is our life, Candy. You're my wife, and just once I'd like to know that you're in my corner, that you're supporting me."

He stopped halfway across the room and crossed his arms. Neil was not a man who kept his distance. He was the one always reaching for her, touching her, refusing to let her bolt and run. This distance between them had happened only once, during a dark period of their life. Tension and uneasiness lingered between them now from the hurtful words he'd thrown in her face.

"What do you want from me, Neil?" she said, and she didn't miss the way his amber eyes seemed to spark with fury. Maybe she'd pushed too hard. Her reasonable Neil seemed to be taking a walk down the wild side, taking him to angry, bitter, resentful places. This wasn't a spot Candy wanted to be in.

"You're my wife, Candy. This isn't about me wanting something from you. I expect you to support me, talk to me, share with me!" He jabbed his thumb to his chest.

"I can't talk to you when you say hurtful things to me, Neil."

He sighed, and maybe he realized he'd gone too far. "I'm sorry. I shouldn't have said what I did, but it's how I feel. I think of it every now and then and wonder how long it would have been before you did end up in his bed. He was in love with you."

She was stunned by the hurt she saw. It was something that could have crumbled any relationship they had. Neil wouldn't have forgiven her for crossing that line. That was just something she knew. Then again, would she have done it?

"I never cheated on you. Jim offered his friendship, but he wasn't and never would have been a man I could love, because I gave everything to you. You can't just pick and choose, Neil. That wasn't something that was going to happen. Neil, you pushed me away. You moved another woman into our home, put her in a bedroom across the hall from ours so that every time I stepped out I could see her, and there you were with her as she carried your baby."

"She was a surrogate, Candy, and I'm sorry, I should never have done that. Why are we talking about this? It's done, it's over."

"Is it? Apparently not, if you're throwing all these feelings you've been holding on to in my face." She held up her hand to stop him so he wouldn't interrupt, which was one of the things he did. "I know I pointed out to you how what you did with Maria was the same as cheating, but I didn't bring it up because I'm still hurt and angry about it or because I think it's still festering between us." She was getting loud, and Neil just watched her closely in a way that let her know she now had all his attention.

"Then why did you throw it in my face, Candy? I'd really like to know. I thought we'd finally gotten past it."

He didn't get it, she realized. He'd missed the point she was trying to make. "I brought it up, Neil, to help you understand that what happened to your mom and dad, the choices they made…they weren't so different from the choices you made with Maria."

He was shaking his head as if there was no way she could convince him, and it was that lack of forgiveness, that hardline attitude, that could end up driving a wedge between his parents and him, ultimately driving them away.

CHAPTER 13

He glanced back in the rearview mirror to Cat in her car seat and Michael beside her, buckled into his. Candy hadn't said a word since climbing into the SUV, since he'd decided he'd tag along with her to his brother's house so she could see her horse and that damn nuisance of a donkey.

"So am I in for the silent treatment all night?" he said. There was something about time and reflecting and looking back on the idiotic things that had flown out of his mouth in the heat of the moment that had him wishing he could go back in time, have a do over. Even with his brother, he felt as if he was putting a wedge between them when Brad was doing nothing more than he would have done in the same situation.

Candy turned to him, and it took her a second before she would look at him. "I just don't know what to say. I've tried to be reasonable, tried to get you to understand, but you're not hearing me, and that hurts, Neil, because you're seeing only your side. That's not who you are. You're an amazing man who's kind and thoughtful at times, but right now I can see you struggling and not willing to understand, and I don't know how else to get through to you," she said, sounding so calm. At the same time, she seemed at a loss for what to say.

"Look, Candy, I'm just trying to get us out of the mess I've got us in. I need to put all my focus into that." Couldn't she get it? He'd ignored things for so long that reality had finally kicked in today while he sat across from that banker, who hadn't been able to see past the black and white numbers to the magic that Neil could create.

"Neil, the money means nothing. If you lost everything, it wouldn't matter to me, because we're more important. All the position, the wealth, success…that's all you. I'm comfortable with a little corner of something. Family is everything, I should know, and if it wasn't for your mom and dad, Neil…" She bit her lip as if she needed to stop herself from saying any more, but he knew where she was heading. She'd already said months before that she would have left if it hadn't been for Brad giving her someone to talk to, and it had been his mom and dad who convinced her to stay.

"Okay, I understand what you're saying, and maybe I'm not able to see it your way. I'm still hurt and can't get my head into understanding yet. Just give me some time, Candy, once I get my head on straight and get us out of this mess. You, Cat, and Michael are my future. Let me just get things settled with us first, take care of us first, and then we'll sit down and talk about my parents."

He was pulling down the driveway to Brad's when he felt Candy reach out and touch his hand. When he glanced over, her understanding reached him.

"Okay," she said. "I get it and I understand, but let me leave you with this, please."

He sighed, just hearing her out.

"Your mom and dad both knew how bad it was between us, how divided we were. The only reason your dad told me that story was because they already knew I had one foot out the door. I'd been seeking out options."

He swallowed his heart. He'd never known for sure how far she had been about to take things in ending their relationship. Now he knew, he guessed. It still ached to know that he'd almost killed the best thing he'd ever created.

"I'm not saying this to hurt you, Neil." She was still touching him as he pulled in and parked beside Emily's minivan and Brad's truck.

He slid around on the seat and took in the honesty in her expression, how she was opening up to him in the one way he'd just accused her of not doing. "I'm listening," he said.

Her smile was so subtle, as if he amused her. "Your dad knew. Your mom had said something to him before she had her stroke. She had been about to reach out, but your dad sat me down at the hospital and explained their story to me. Your mom had him tell me everything when she was in rehab. She was humiliated and embarrassed, and I can see still how she has to struggle with that memory, wishing she could go back and undo that moment and make a different choice, but she can't, just like none of us can. She explained, and your dad did, too, that it's not about what they did then. It's about who they are now. They're good people, Neil. They're your parents, and they're the reason I'm here, that I stayed, that I chose to work it out. It was because of their mistakes and their heartache that I could understand how that could have been our story. It could have been us."

This time, he wanted to argue, but she reached over again and stopped him. "Just think about it, Neil.

Remember who your mom is, your dad, and forget what you heard. She deserves your respect, and she and your dad will always have mine—and my gratitude. You know about their story, but this is really about you and your issues." She jabbed her finger to his chest, maybe to drive her point home. "You never told me what happened with the bank yesterday." She looked away, letting him know she'd said her peace and was leaving him to think about what he needed to say, to do.

No, he hadn't. He was just glad she hadn't been there to witness that banker cutting him down and making him feel as if he needed to get his house in order before knocking on his door. It had been humbling.

"I can tell it didn't go well," she said.

He was shaking his head as he turned off the ignition and pulled the keys out, watching the tractor in the distance coming closer, realizing it was Brad driving with earmuffs on for the noise. "No, it didn't. I had high hopes, but I was dealing with a drone who saw how bad a hole I'd managed to sink us in." The resort was in flux, and Neil had turned over the day-to-day operations to the prospective owner, but he realized it was time to have his own people watching over things. "I should have called Stella. We haven't talked in a while, but she knows me, understands me. I was just trying to get us something here until we go back." He drummed his fingers on the steering wheel, thinking, and glanced over to Candy. She was staring straight ahead out the window.

"Neil, just don't forget about me. You tend to start making plans and thinking, and you bulldoze straight ahead to the finish line but forget to tell me, leaving me trying to figure out where you've gone to. So please, first, there are some things that need to happen before considering a trip back—like our family, our home here, and your feelings for your mother." She gave him a meaningful look before pulling open the door and slipping out just as Emily started out of the house, all smiles. She headed over to Candy and gave her a big-sisterly hug.

Neil realized as he watched her that Candy now had a family, his family, and she'd set down roots here. Maybe this was about him being the selfish one once again.

CHAPTER 14

Neil watched as Emily and Candy disappeared in the distance to the pasture just behind the break in the trees where the horses were grazing. He'd left Michael and Cat inside the house with Katy, Brad and Emily's eldest, who was now fifteen, filling out into a beautiful young lady. He wondered how long it would be before the boys came knocking on her door.

It was an image that made him smile, considering Brad would be the type to lay down the law with whatever boy came sniffing around. He'd soon learn that he wouldn't be messing with Brad's kids, especially Katy. Neil watched Brad climb down from the tractor, the bales of hay stacked on the flatbed behind it. He pulled off his earmuffs and looped them on the steering wheel of the tractor, and he seemed to hesitate a second as he took in Neil. Maybe he was wondering what to say, considering Neil had acted like a complete ass when he had come by earlier.

He was walking toward him, digging into each step. "So what brings you by?" Brad asked, sounding a little annoyed.

"Candy wanted to see her horse and donkey."

Brad didn't seem impressed. Maybe there was more.

"And I wanted to eat a little crow and apologize for being…"

Brad stopped in front of him, not about to make this easy. No, he was making it damn hard, but then, he'd had it coming. "I'm waiting, Neil."

Great, so his brother was going to make him grovel. "I took out my frustration on you and on Candy when the only one to blame for the situation I'm in is me." He didn't miss the surprise in Brad's expression, but there was humor, too.

"Can't believe you had it in you." He reached out and rested his hand on Neil's shoulder. "So how about the loan I offered? I know you'd do the same."

It was true, but there was something about taking money this way. He couldn't do it.

"Come on, Neil," Brad said. "This isn't the time to let your pride kick in. I understand better than anyone." He glanced over at the sound of the horses, spotting Emily and Candy with two of them saddled. Emily was astride a small paint, and Candy was riding her big boy, Sable, the gray Azteca. His long main had been brushed, and Neil wondered why Candy was so adamant about keeping it long, especially out here in the rain and the mud. It was always a mess every time she came by.

"Where're you two off to?" Brad said as Candy turned Sable easily and Emily worked at it a little more. They were both in jeans. Candy had a dark sweater pulled over her shirt, and Emily was wearing a light jacket and a ball cap. Candy had tied her hair back in a messy bun to keep the hair from her eyes.

"Just a quick ride to exercise Sable," she said. "Talked Emily into tagging along. Thought we'd do the loop. It's just a short ride." She patted Sable's neck. Neil wasn't surprised, because he knew Candy better than she knew herself at times. When it came to Sable, she had a hard time staying off him. She'd more often than not throw her leg over and mount him and ride bareback as soon as she got here.

"Candy, don't go out any longer," Neil said, and Brad looked to him, then back to Emily and Candy.

"Em, be careful on him," Brad said. "He's been a little spooky lately. I'm not kidding—don't go any farther. It's getting late, and I don't want either of you out riding when the sun's going down."

Neil couldn't help wondering if there was something else, as Brad sounded overly worried, which was unlike him.

"Maybe they shouldn't go out," Neil said. "Candy!"

She turned again.

"Maybe it's not such a good idea, this late. How about in the morning? We'll come back and you can both go out."

"What?" Candy said, circling Sable, who seemed a little antsy. "Neil, Brad, you both are being ridiculous. We'll be back in an hour or sooner, but these guys need some exercise." Candy could be stubborn sometimes, and Neil started toward her, about to reach out and grab the halter and make her get down, but Brad reached out and touched his chest.

"She's right. They need exercise," he said, then waved to his wife, who was looking to Candy and then him. "Em, you just follow Candy. Keep it slow, no racing out there."

Emily just rolled her eyes as they turned their horses and started to the trailhead at the back of the property, which led into forested public land.

"Well, since you're here and it seems my wife is off

with yours, why don't you tell me some more about your plans for your business, see if I can help in some way?" Brad looped his arm around Neil's shoulders and started him to the house. "Katy watching the kids?"

"She is at that. Got to tell you, Brad, it won't be long before you have your hands full with her and the boys come knocking." He strode into the back door, hearing the kids in the living room and seeing Katy in the kitchen, Michael perched on her hip and the phone to her ear.

"Who're you talking to, Katy?" Brad said from behind him.

"I've got to go. It's my dad," Katy said before hanging up. "Jason," she said.

Brad looked over to Neil as he kicked off his mud-covered boots. "Afraid it's already started," he said.

CHAPTER 15

At first, Neil didn't recognize the idea he came up with while sitting with Brad, feet up in the living room, while Katy did her homework at the coffee table. Trevor was reading a graphic novel, wearing dark-rimmed glasses in the easy chair, his feet dangling over the side. Cat and Becky were playing with dolls, and Michael was reorganizing all the dresses and Barbie furniture the girls had set up in the big doll house in the corner of the living room.

"So this guy buying the resort was the same person we met when we were all in Cancun for Mom and Dad's anniversary?" Brad asked.

"Same company, father–son team. The father owns a number of resorts already in Puerto Vallarta, Cabo, and Laredo. They wanted to add mine. It would be a great fit, considering mine is five stars, but it's on the higher end of what they're used to. It was part of this timeshare exchange they're involved in," Neil said. "It's not that they haven't given me anything, because they have. The deposit in trust with Stella, my banker in Cancun, is there at least to keep it afloat and pay the operating expenses. The problem is this guy could walk at any time before paying the full amount I'm asking, and he's been dragging his feet."

"Well, let me just put this out there," Brad said. "Not that I'm saying it's a done deal, but sounds to me he's been on the fence long enough. You know resorts. It was your dream to have it. Why not take it back but maybe bring in some partners to run it? You need operating capital, so bring in others who can provide that, and, as you just said, you want to think long and hard about uprooting Candy again with the kids. If you go back to Cancun full time, move there, run your resort, will Candy be okay with that, or can you run something from here?"

"In a perfect world, I'd be in both places, here and Cancun, going back and forth. I think Candy would like that, and seeing her with Em, the kids here together…I've never seen her so settled and happy. Even with you, big brother. I know she really looks forward to all the time we spend together, the first real family she's ever had. It'd be tough to take that away, and if I moved us back there…"

"You're afraid she'll be unhappy?" Brad was leaning forward, resting his elbows on his knees.

"There're a lot of bad memories there. Being here gave us the distance I needed from the surrogate, and Candy, too. I know she'd go back, but living here has her more settled, more confident and happier, even though she misses Mom and Dad." He sighed, because listening to Candy and hearing her try to get through to him about his mom and what had happened, he wondered whether he'd taken too hard a line. Candy was obviously more understanding than him.

Brad had an odd look on his face and then shook his

head. Maybe he and Brad really did need to sit down and talk about what they'd learned.

"Dad, what time is Mom coming back?" Katy looked up from where she was writing in her notebook.

Brad stood up and looked out the window, then at his watch. "Any time now. Maybe they're putting the horses away." Brad wandered into the kitchen and then looked out the back door. Neil could hear the springs squeak on the screen. "Em!" he called out, and Neil wandered up behind him and slipped on his boots.

No one answered, and it was that silence that worried Neil. The sun was dropping lower in the sky, and it was getting close to dinner time. They'd now been out for about an hour and a half. Nothing to worry about yet, but the way his brother had harped at Emily earlier and was now walking out the door concerned him.

"Hey, what's going on?" Neil called out just as Brad pulled his cell phone from his back pocket. He was shaking his head. "Em, where are you? Answer the damn phone. Call me back. I'm starting to get a little worried." Brad hung up. "It went to voicemail." He shook his head again.

"Okay, now you're starting to freak me out a bit. What's going on? They've been gone this long before. What's up?" he said.

"I don't know, just a feeling I had earlier and couldn't shake. Springtime, you know. Maybe I'm making too much of it. It's just that Em not answering doesn't ease my mind." He held up the phone.

"What is it you're worried about?" Neil asked. "They were taking the loop—nice, easy, flat. Should be no problems."

Brad didn't say anything as he glanced back once at Neil. "Out here with miles of public land, wilderness and nothing else, they could run into just about anything. The fact that they should have been back by now makes me more uneasy than ever. You never know what's out in the spring, a mother bear and her cubs, cougars… Could be anything."

Okay, now Brad was making him worry, and Brad was the one in the family who didn't panic. "Maybe we should go and look for them," Neil said, and Brad looked to the house and the screen door that squeaked open.

"Dad, we're getting hungry," Katy said. "What should I do about dinner? Mom has a stew in the crockpot."

Brad glanced to Neil. "You stay here with the kids," he said. "I'll go look for the girls." He started back into the house for his coat, but Neil looked out at the horizon, at the miles of trees, and said, "No, let's call your neighbor June, have her come and stay with the kids. I'm going with you."

CHAPTER 16

Candy loved riding her horse. Being on Sable was truly a magical experience for her. There was something about this time, riding in this part of the country, far away from city life. Even Cancun, with her sandy beach and oceanfront property, had nothing on the beauty of this area. She led their horses on the miles of trails back here. Trees surrounded them: cedar, fir, and some maple. There was undergrowth, too, and there was something different every time even though she rode this trail so often she believed she could do it in her sleep.

Emily was behind her on the paint she loved to ride, Trudy. She glanced back a number of times and circled around, but there was something about Trudy today, the way she kept pinning her ears back every time Candy and Sable got too close.

"Would you stop it, already? You're being silly. We ride together all the time. You guys are supposed to be friends," Emily said to the horse, and Candy wanted to laugh because Emily at times talked to the horse as she did her own children.

"Could be just the pecking order. I have a feeling Ambrose may have thrown it off a bit," Emily said. Trudy had once been closer to the bottom, but there was something about Ambrose and Sable together that made them rank closer to Lucy, the quarter horse and lead mare that Brad always rode. "I'm glad you came out with me, Em. I always feel so much better after I go out for a ride. Kind of clears my head and helps me to shake off everything that's bothering me."

"How's it going with Neil? I have to tell you, Brad has been worried. Me, too. We love having you both so close, but this small-town life…we're starting to think it's pulling Neil down."

Hearing Emily voice what she already knew didn't help or make her feel any better. She was about to say something more about Neil when she stopped, remembering how much it bothered him to have her talking to Brad and Emily about everything that was happening with them.

"He's figuring it out," she said as she found the dip in the path to take them down the bank and across the meadow to the trail going back. She chirped and turned Sable, leading him down through the thick brush and then pulling him to a stop when a downed tree blocked their path. "Emily, I don't think we can get around this." She climbed down just as Emily pulled up the paint.

"That wasn't here before," Emily said.

It was a large tree caught in a big cedar, and there was no way they could go over it, as it was at the height of her head. She could crawl under it, but there was no way she'd get her horse down and through. She grabbed the halter of the paint, who was getting antsy. "We're going to have to turn around. We can't get through this way."

Emily wasn't the most confident of riders, and she still had to learn that when she worried, her horse would pick up on her stress. That became a problem for less confident riders, who could suddenly find themselves unable to control their horses.

"We'll just turn around and go back the way we came, no big deal. Do you think you can do some trotting?" She could easily do a canter with Sable, and a gallop, too, but she knew Emily didn't like running the horses. She was more comfortable at a walk. When trotting, she still bounced a lot and grabbed the saddle horn.

"As long as it's not too fast, and if I say stop, can you?" The paint backed up and bumped the branches, then pranced sideways. "Whoa, Trudy!"

"Emily, it's fine. You're doing good. Just take her back off this trail to the one we just came off, and then I'll go ahead of you." She was doing her best to keep Emily calm, and she slid her foot in the stirrup and had just climbed up when there was a noise. The paint whinnied and took off. Emily yelled.

"Trudy, stop!" Candy shouted. She had her leg over and moved Sable, jumping the dip in the path and heading up the embankment after Emily, who was on a runaway Trudy.

"Em, pull the rein back, one rein past your knee! Keep it low," she called out, moving Sable fast and hard, leaning forward to urge him on.

Emily was screaming and pulling the rein, and Trudy went to the side and slowed, prancing and skittish. When Candy reached Emily, she leaned forward to grab the reins just as she stopped Sable.

"Oh my God, I'm shaking," Emily said. "She's never done this before. Something spooked her. I hate it when Brad is right at times. Just don't tell him."

Candy just smiled, trying to get Emily to calm down when she heard a sound that had the hair on the back of her neck going up. Sable bolted, and Candy lost her balance, falling back. It was then that everything went into slow motion. Emily's eyes went wide, someone yelled, a horse screamed, and she hit the ground, her head snapping back. Her breath left her in a whoosh.

CHAPTER 17

Brad had just finished saddling his quarter horse, sliding his rifle in behind the saddle, and throwing extra shells in his saddlebag when his cell phone rang. Neil was putting the bridle on the black Arabian he loved to ride.

Brad pulled out his phone. "It's Em." He came around the back of the horse, holding the bridle. "Where the hell are you?" he barked. The only thing Neil could hear was the panic in Emily's voice, but he couldn't make out what she was saying.

"She fell," Brad said, gesturing to Neil. Brad had all his attention.

"Who fell?"

"Tell me where you are," Brad said, then tilted the phone away from his mouth. "Candy fell. Her horse spooked. Emily can't get to her." He slipped the bridle on and looped the reins over the mare's neck. "We're coming to you. Keep your phone on and stay there. I know where you are." Brad was nodding into the phone as if Emily could see him. Whatever she was saying, she was totally freaked out, and Neil was ready to yell at Brad to hurry up. "I don't care about the damn horse at this point. Tie her up to a branch, but get off her. Stay right there. I'll find you."

Brad slid the phone in his pocket and was in the saddle. "The girls had to turn back about three quarters of the way at the turnoff. There was a tree down. They couldn't get past it, and the paint spooked and got away from Emily. Dammit, I knew it. I know she loves that horse, but it's too much of a horse for her. Candy stopped her, and then Sable spooked, threw Candy, and took off. Em's already called 911, and Search and Rescue are heading in. She called them right before me. She said Candy isn't moving. She may have hit her head."

Brad kicked up his horse and moved, Neil right behind him. He was scared of the unknown, and Candy…how bad was she hurt? This was the fear he had of her riding, getting hurt even though she was so comfortable in a saddle, on a horse. Her being thrown wasn't something he'd expected.

"What else did Emily say, Brad?" he shouted as he squeezed the sides of the horse and pulled up behind him.

Brad didn't look back as he took a corner in the trail fast. "I don't know. Emily was freaked out about hearing something, could be a cougar. Let's just get out there."

There were shadows everywhere as the sun dropped lower, and this was the first time Neil had ever seen Brad push a horse as hard as he was. Neil couldn't get past the horror that something had happened to Candy. This was a kind of fear he'd never experienced before. Even when they'd survived the storm together, she had been with him. He was so angry that his body ached from the worry. The only thing he prayed he'd have the chance to do was put his hands on her, spitting mad, and kiss her.

"HEY, you, I can't believe how much fun this is. Such a great idea." She was floating in the water. Looking back at the shore, she could see Michael and Cat playing in the sand.

"I didn't think you'd want to come back here. I'm so glad you did. I saved this part for you, part of your ocean, your beach. That was where your house was before the storm took it down."

She stood up in the soft blue as the waves slapped against her legs. The warm ocean water was so inviting, and the sun shone down on Candy and on Neil, bare chested in swim trunks as he raced back to Michael and lifted him in the air, then dipped him in the water. He giggled as Neil splashed his legs. It was picture perfect. Her children were having so much fun, and Neil lay down in the sand with Michael on top of him, and she just stood there, watching, dipping her hand in the water and taking another step, feeling the warmth of the sun beating down. She looked down the beach to the building, the resort that was now where her tiny house used to be, her father's house before the storm took it down. It was beautiful. She didn't know why she had been scared, why she had worried. It didn't make sense, because being here with Neil, with Cat, with Michael seemed so right. Why had she fought this?

She went to take another step, but she couldn't move. Her foot was stuck. It was heavy. She saw the shadow, and it was coming from the estate, the path Neil always walked, always, before coming to her. It was *her*, her dark hair pinned back to the sides of her round face, her eyes dark. She was wearing a peach bikini top and a white skirt that wrapped around her waist and knotted on the side. She'd always had a full body, hips that were made to carry a child, and she was walking right to Neil, clapping her hands, not even looking her way but smiling down at Michael, who raced toward her as fast as his little legs could, calling out, "Mama!" She lifted him in the air, kissed him, and hugged him before looking back at Neil. She was barefoot as she walked toward him, her belly round—Maria, Michael's mother. She reached Neil, and he leaned down and kissed her, touching her pregnant belly. This wasn't right. She was standing right here, and where were her kids? Then she heard a voice, yelling, calling to her: "Candy! Answer me…" It was an echo, but it wasn't Neil, and he wasn't looking. He was on the beach, laughing with the children, his children.

She gasped. Her eyes were open, and she didn't know where she was as she struggled, trying to get a breath again and again. It was the worst, the panic of not being able to suck in a breath as she clawed at her shirt, her neck. Then she heard more yelling, heard gravel and rocks falling. Emily was beside her on the ground, touching her and reaching for her hand. As Candy felt the panic, she grasped at her chest and pounded.

"Calm down. Take a breath, slow and steady. You're gasping and panicking. Stop, don't fight it. Slow down." Emily sounded so calm, and Candy finally got a breath, then took another, slower.

"Are you hurt? You scared the hell out of me," Emily said.

Candy took in the dribble of blood above Emily's eye and the dimness of the night. "Where's Sable?" Her voice sounded off. She didn't recognize it. It sounded so strange to her own ears. "It was a cougar, that cry, wasn't it?" She remembered that horrible sound and the feeling of eyes watching her. She had been sucked back to that horrible dream.

"He took off," Emily said. "I'm more worried about you. You fell down the embankment, you weren't moving. I called Brad. He's coming."

She wanted to move, and she started to roll to her side. "Help me up," she said, reaching for Emily's hand and rolling over, feeling stiff and sore.

"I don't know if that's a good idea. You could be hurt bad. You didn't answer me. You landed really hard, Candy."

She couldn't calm Emily down as she struggled to sit up. Then she heard Brad shouting, calling out to Emily.

"Down here!" Emily yelled back, and Candy somehow held on to Emily as she started to sit up. She almost threw up, her head was dizzy. She must have swayed, as Emily slid her arm around her and let her lean against her.

"Candy!" It was Neil shouting, and she could hear the men sliding down. She blinked again, taking in the trees and the hill. Did her head hurt? She was dizzy. It was such a relief then that they were there.

"Are you hurt?" Neil was on his knees, and Brad, too, touching her and Emily and hovering. It was welcome, even though she was so confused.

"Just my pride. I can't believe I got thrown," she said as Neil pulled her closer and she cried out. "Ouch, my shoulder."

Neil was looking at her, running his hands over her, holding her face. Then he looked at his hand. "You're bleeding, Candy. You have blood on the back of your head."

She reached back to touch, but he grabbed her hand.

"Don't touch," he said. "You probably need stitches."

"Well, just help me up. Have you seen Sable, Neil, was he there?" She couldn't believe he would just take off.

"Do we chance moving her?" Brad said, and Emily was talking, too. Everyone was talking, and she just wanted them to stop. The kids would need her. She couldn't stay here.

Neil was running his hands down her back, over her arms. "Candy, where are you hurt?"

"I'm okay." She had to clear her throat. "Just help me up."

Neil held her still. "Search and Rescue are on their way. I don't know if that's such a good idea."

"I've fallen harder, Neil. I'm fine. Just help me up."

Neil stood up and put his arm around her waist, pulling her up to him, holding her. For a second, she swayed as she rested her head against his shoulder, against him, his hand holding her to him.

"She okay?" Brad asked behind her, and she felt another hand touching her, but she didn't want to nod.

"Enough, just help me up the hill," she said. As they started up, she watched Brad help Emily. She was climbing up, using her hands, pulling at roots. Brad had his hand on her bum, pushing her. Neil was still there, holding Candy.

"Ready?" he said, taking in the hill. She could see he was trying to assess how to get her up, and she couldn't help looking at him and all his handsomeness. He really was a catch. "I love you," she said to him, and he gave her an odd look.

"I know you do." He seemed worried. "You scared the hell out of me, Candy."

She just looked at him and then started up the hill, her husband behind her, helping her up. Then she heard it again, that chilling sound, and Brad grabbed his rifle from behind his saddle, pointed it into the woods, and fired.

CHAPTER 18

The fire was going in the bedroom, and Candy could hear Neil down the hall, tucking in Michael. She was still shaken from their little ride and how horribly wrong the night had gone. They were lucky nothing more had happened, and Candy had escaped with three stitches in the back of her head, a mild concussion, and a bruise on her shoulder that would cause her some grief over the next few days.

What had shaken Emily was the cougar that had been hunting them. When Brad shot the cat, it had landed just behind the horses, and he'd tossed it over Trudy's back, then pulled his wife up with him and led the paint behind them. Candy had ridden behind Neil, her hands around his waist, resting her head against his back as he rode home.

Brad had called Search and Rescue on his cell phone to let them know they'd found the women, and even though Neil was furious that Candy had been hurt, she'd been relieved to see Sable outside the barn, waiting, when they rode in. He definitely knew where home was. Neil had left the horses for Brad to unsaddle, carrying Candy to the SUV and then taking her to the hospital. Brad had swung by with the kids to drop them off after Candy was patched up, checked over, and sent home from the emergency room.

"Hey, how's your head?" Neil asked as he strode in, still wearing a serious look. He hadn't smiled once that night.

"Doesn't hurt anymore. The pills worked a little too well," she said, resting against the three plumped pillows behind her.

"You scared the hell out of me tonight." He looked away as he sat beside her on the bed, and when he looked back, she had to reach over and touch his hand.

"Scared me, too. I didn't stop to think about a cougar. It being spring time, with the sun going down, it was prime hunting time. Shouldn't have been riding that late in the day, I guess," she said.

"Well, you're off the horse for a while. You have a concussion, Candy. Maybe it's time you think about wearing a helmet."

She couldn't believe he of all people would say that. "Look, Neil, it was a freak thing that happened. Emily's horse got away from her, and I was trying to catch her and hold her. I was caught off guard. I'd never lose my seat normally. I think Emily just needs a gentler horse until she becomes more confident."

Neil was already shaking his head. "Oh, I'm pretty sure Brad's putting an end to her riding for the next little bit, anyway."

That didn't surprise her. Brad, Neil, Jed, and even Andy were so overprotective, and something like this would push all of their protective instincts. She should have felt comforted, protected, but she couldn't shake where her head had gone, what she had dreamed while unconscious.

It had been an illusion, she didn't know what, but it had seemed so real, and it haunted her. She wanted to weep, thinking of the woman who had turned her life, her feelings, and almost her marriage upside down.

"What's wrong?" Neil asked, facing her and reaching out, touching her face.

She took a minute to just look at her husband watching her. She'd kept so much in for so long, putting all her hurt, her insecurities, her feelings into that journal and keeping it from him. "When I fell, I had this dream." She was watching to see if he would dismiss her, but he didn't look away. His expression was, if anything, that of a man interested in what she had to say. "We were back in Cancun, at my beach. I was standing in the ocean, and you were there, too, with Michael and Cat playing in the sand. It was so nice and warm, and I missed it."

His expression didn't change, and he appeared to be thinking, but instead of talking or taking over the conversation, he listened.

"Then there was something off. I got this unsettled feeling, a sadness, looking at your resort where my house used to be, Dad's house. Everything of mine was gone, wiped away as if it had never existed. Then I saw her." She watched Neil closely for his reaction, and she could tell he was wondering, but he still said nothing as he continued to touch her leg. "Maria."

"Seriously, Candy?" Neil pulled away and went to stand up, but she didn't want him to dismiss her, not over this.

"Neil, this is important. You talked about me not sharing, so I'm sharing." She touched his arm, and this time when he glanced back at her, she realized that Maria brought out a vulnerability in Neil that she'd never seen before. "She was walking toward you, toward the water, wearing a bikini and a skirt, dressed for the beach. She was happy, smiling, and Michael saw her and ran to her. He knew who she was, and he called her Mama, and he was so happy. Then you walked toward her, and she was pregnant again with your child, another child. I was calling to you, and you didn't answer. You kissed her, and you were so happy, and my heart was breaking even though it wasn't real…but it seemed to be."

She just watched as he tried to digest what she was saying. He reached out and slid his hand over her cheek, allowing her to lean in.

"You look at me, Candy Friessen. There isn't a chance in hell I could ever be happy without you. There's no other woman, there can never be another woman. You are and will always be Michael's mother. I'd walk through fire for you and walk away from everything for us."

It was the tears in his eyes, the passion for her as he leaned in, pressing his head to hers, that told her it was time to let go of the fear she'd been holding on to for so long.

She said, "I know."

CHAPTER 19

He'd hovered most of the night, listening to Candy breathe in and out, her soft moans as she turned in her sleep. In the morning, he helped her up for a hot bath as she stiffened. She was lying down again, sleeping, just as Neil finished up a second cup of coffee and had the kids playing quietly, Cat with her dolls and Michael with his big toy box, filled with an abundance of toys that would occupy him for the next little bit.

What Candy had shared had kept waking him. She had voiced her worst fears through her dream. He didn't believe in premonitions or anything like that, but he did believe that she'd mixed up a whole bunch of things and pictured an outcome that would destroy her, a fear that she couldn't shake. That was something he'd done to her. It was a picture that had rolled through his mind over and over repeatedly through the night, and by morning he swore he'd do anything to help her get to a place where she'd never, ever have to worry about Maria again.

Her fears were real, so he needed to find a way to reassure her it couldn't happen—it wouldn't happen. He had his children, Cat and Michael. He had a wife he loved more than his next breath, a woman who couldn't be replaced because she was the one in every sense, even though he'd once tried to mold her, before and after they were married, into someone she wasn't.

It hadn't been realistic, because Candy was complicated, thoughtful, deeply devoted, intuitive, quiet at times, filled with passion. She didn't fit in with the black-tie crowd and couldn't cook if her life depended on it. He smiled at that thought. How could he get her to believe that all her quirks and everything about her that made them both compatible and not in so many ways also made her the perfect woman for him?

She challenged him, she excited him, and he couldn't live without her.

There was a knock at the door, and Neil hurried over before it woke Candy. He pulled it open to see Brad and Emily with the kids.

"Hey, guys, come on in," he said. He ruffled the girls' hair and Trevor's as they passed, and of course Michael and Cat were excited to see their cousins. Katy lifted Michael, who blabbered away in his baby talk to her, and little Becky was talking to Cat. Then they were both on the floor with their dolls.

"How're you doing, Emily?" He touched her shoulders and looked at the cut above her eye, which had to have come from a bush or stick while she made her way down the hill to Candy.

"Just tired is all, but we were worried about Candy."

Brad looked a little worse for wear, and he stepped inside, taking Emily's coat from her and tossing it over the chair. Trevor was hanging his in the closet. "Trevor, go and play with the girls," Brad said.

"They're playing with dolls, Dad. I don't play with Barbies."

Neil nearly laughed at the comment. "Don't blame you, Trevor. Why don't you go in my office and play on my computer if your dad says it's okay? I have that Star Wars videogame you love."

"Oh, thanks, Uncle Neil!" Trevor sounded so excited as he started across the room to the back of the house, where Neil's office was.

"Hey, Trevor, your uncle said only if it was okay with me. Did you ask me yet?" Brad called out to him, and Trevor stopped and turned.

"Oops, sorry, Dad. Can I?" he asked.

"Yeah, go, but just the game, no YouTube," he called out as Trevor hurried away before Brad could change his mind again.

"Sorry, I thought considering we're all a little tired, it would be okay," Neil said. "There's still coffee. Do either of you want any?" he asked.

"Sure, could always use another," Brad said.

"None for me, Neil," Emily said just as there was a squeak on the stairs.

Candy was coming down, wearing black sweatpants and a white long-sleeved T-shirt. She was moving slowly, and her hair was tucked behind her ears, hanging straight down her back. It was a mess, and she looked absolutely gorgeous. She was carrying a brush as she stepped off the last step barefoot, looking exhausted and beautiful at the same time. "Thought I heard you two." She was moving slowly, being stiff and sore. She couldn't hide it from Neil.

"You want me to brush your hair?" Neil was touching her and holding her elbow.

She slid her arm around his waist and leaned against him, maybe to steady herself. "No, I'll get Emily to. If you wouldn't mind getting me a coffee, it may help clear my head a bit."

"Of course," Emily said, taking the brush. Candy didn't move for another second, then took a breath before pushing away from him. She did glance up, and he could tell too by the frown that her head was hurting. "How about another Advil?" Neil said.

"Yeah." She smiled, looking over at him, and he didn't miss the shell-shocked expression on Emily's face.

"You scared me to death, Candy," Emily said, tapping the brush in her palm.

Brad was watching both women and then looking over to the children as if he wouldn't let anyone out of his sight. "You're both lucky you weren't hurt worse," he said. "Candy, you may be a good rider, but things happen out on the trail. I knew I should have put my foot down and said no, it wasn't a good time to go out."

Candy was looking at Neil. He wasn't sure what she was thinking, as her expression softened as she looked over to Brad. Emily just shut her eyes as if she'd already heard this lecture.

"Maybe you're right, Brad, but we're okay. All's well," Candy said.

For a minute, Neil watched his brother and wondered whether he was going to add something else.

"You're lucky is all, Candy. Last night could very well have had a very different outcome. One with either of you…" Brad stopped, and Neil stepped in and pressed his hand to Candy's lower back.

"Go sit down and I'll get you some coffee, Brad," Neil said. He was just as tired and frustrated, but this wasn't the time. Once, he'd have lit into Candy, but listening to her open up the night before to him after finding her lying in the woods with blood on the back of her head, it had been humbling and had scared the hell out of him.

Neil walked into the kitchen and pulled out two more mugs, then splashed coffee in one for Candy and the other for Brad.

"Sounds like you got about as much sleep as I did," Neil added as Brad grunted and picked up the milk carton to dump some in his mug. Neil handed him a spoon, which he took.

"I yelled at Emily last night," Brad said as he stirred and set the spoon in a puddle of spilled coffee on the counter. He took a swallow, standing off to the side where they could see into the living room. Candy was perched on the sectional, her arm resting over the back of a cushion, and Emily was brushing her hair carefully. She'd have to be mindful of the stitches.

"Can understand why. I would've yelled at Candy if it accomplished anything, but it wouldn't have. They're okay, Brad. They're home." He stepped around Brad and didn't miss him wince at whatever he'd been thinking as Neil carried Candy's coffee out and handed it to her. She took it, offering him a smile in thanks.

Brad was still watching the women and the kids as he drank, his hand resting on his hip. He was wearing blue jeans and a faded green T-shirt. "I'm surprised at you, Neil. You're rather calm. I thought you of anyone would have laid down the law with Candy. You seem unusually supportive."

"Have you to thank for that," he said as he stood beside his brother. He didn't miss how confused Brad seemed.

"You lost me, Neil. How am I responsible for you suddenly becoming reasonable?"

Neil wanted to laugh. "Oh, I'd say it's brotherly love lately and the fact you've been my wife's closest confidant, telling me in not so many words that I've pushed too hard with her. Last night was the first time she opened up to me instead of running off to her journal and writing down her feelings, her thoughts, her worries, or confiding in you. She talked to me."

He wondered whether Brad understood. Maybe he did, as his expression softened as he stared out at his family and Candy and Emily, who were chatting together. His wife was still brushing Candy's hair. Emily loved her. They were sisters.

"What did you do with the cougar?" Neil poured himself another coffee with what was left and decided to make another pot.

"She's hanging in the shed. Going to skin her, turn her into a rug, maybe stick her in our room to remind Emily of the years she took off me." He took another sip, and Neil wondered for a second whether he was serious.

"A little harsh, don't you think?" He had never seen Brad this upset before.

"Maybe, just give me some time. Emily isn't as horse smart as Candy, and look what happened out there. I go into a sweat every time I see that cat because I know it could have killed one of them," Brad said.

Neil had feared the same thing, but every time he started to think of what could have happened, he forced his thoughts somewhere else. He took in the gray that was coming in heavier at the sides of Brad's head. Maybe a few more had popped up the night before. "You know it'll be damn near impossible to keep Candy off a horse and Emily from going with her," Neil said.

Brad didn't say anything for the longest time. "I know, which is why I'm getting rid of that paint and finding her a gentler mount she can handle. I'll spend more time riding with her until I know she's steadier, more confident. She's

too green. She didn't grow up with horses like we did."
There was such love there. Brad didn't even try to hide
how much Emily meant to him. "So I wanted to give you
this. I know we never got to the money thing when we were
talking last night." Brad pulled out a folded check from his
pocket and held it between his fingers to Neil, and he could
see Candy watching. She had to know what Brad was
doing. "I planned to give it to you then."

Neil opened the check, looking at the amount, and he
was a little stunned. It should have made him happy. It was
fifty thousand dollars and would tide them over for a while,
but the way he was being handed money left him with an
uneasy feeling. He handed the check back to Brad. "You
know what? I can't take this. As much as I need this and
could use it, I can't take money from you this way."

Brad raised his hand and backed away. He refused to
take it back, giving Neil his "Don't be an idiot" look.

"I had a lot of time to think last night," Neil said, "and
one of the things I realized had to do with my business
plan."

Brad was looking confused, and Neil looked over to
Candy and Emily, who were sitting there quietly.

He cleared his throat to get Emily and Candy's attention. "What I'm proposing is turning the Cancun resort
into a Friessen family business."

As Neil looked around the room, the kids looked up at
him, and the shock on Emily's and Candy's faces gave way
to surprise.

Brad seemed to consider something before nodding.
"Okay, show us the plan."

CHAPTER 20

"Candy, I have an idea about some of the changes." Neil was holding papers, reading something as he walked into the bedroom, where she was sitting in the easy chair, her feet up on the ottoman, reading a book. He appeared to be confused or thinking about something as he stared at her from the middle of the room.

"Yes?" she said, giving him all her attention.

He was looking around the room and then over to the door. He tossed the outline of his business plan on the bed. It was ten pages stapled together, and there appeared to be notes in the margins in pen. What was he up to now? He gestured in the air and said, "I'll be right back."

Then he was gone, and Candy was looking at the door, wondering what big ideas he'd come up with.

"Neil, what are you doing?" Candy started to get up and reached for his plan on the bed, but to her, this stuff made no sense. She wasn't a business major, and Candy, unlike Neil, had gone to school down in Mexico. Her classes had leaned toward the basics: reading, writing, and math. She hadn't gone to college or university, and she didn't have a degree. Candy had learned about surviving, getting by and working with her two hands.

Neil clapped his hands and rubbed them together when he strode back in, this time with a baby monitor attached to his pocket. "Okay, where was I?" he said as he took the monitor so they could hear Michael and set it on the dresser before reaching for the papers Candy was holding. She was trying to make sense of his notes.

"Ah, yes, there it is." Neil flipped a page, and she looked over his arm, curious as to what he was up to. "I want to run something by you," he said, flipping over another page and showing her a list of names. She noted Andy's, Brad's, and Jed's, and below that hers, Emily's, Diana's, and Laura's.

"What are you up to now?" She couldn't help being curious and excited about something that included all of them.

"You know how I mentioned downstairs earlier when Brad and Emily came by about the Friessen family resort? I outlined a rough plan to Brad where I mentioned having him, Andy, and Jed partner with me. I would sell them shares, and we'd become equal shareholders, because you know I have no intention of taking handouts from my brother."

She rubbed his shoulder, because she understood his thinking, understood where he was coming from. "I like the idea, Neil. I already told you that." She did like the idea of having his brothers and Andy together in business to watch his back, and she sensed it would maybe help to keep everyone grounded while providing the influx of cash Neil needed to run the operation. It would also add some legitimacy to their arrangement. More than that, there was something about this idea of having all the Friessen men as part of this, as if they would close ranks and eliminate

Candy's fear of returning to Cancun. She couldn't explain it or put it into words that made sense.

"The only problem I'm having with this idea is the possibility of butting heads. We all need a vote, but there needs to be someone running it, leading the board, keeping it so that our resort stays in the family."

She was nodding because she understood what he was saying, but she still didn't quite get why hers and the other women's names were there. "I think everyone would agree you should oversee it. After all, this is where you shine. I'm confused as to why you have my name there, and Emily's, Diana's, and Laura's? You know I don't understand business. Diana I can see, with her being a lawyer, but Laura's never even finished high school, and Emily has always just been a mom. How is it you think we can add something?"

Neil rested his hands on her shoulders. "Sit down. Come on, I want to talk to you about this."

Candy allowed Neil to arrange her and sit her down in the chair while he sat on the ottoman, reaching for her legs and resting them over his. "You know the ranch, Brad and Emily's, used to belong to Dad and his father before that. The way Granddad willed it, it would go to the eldest son."

Candy was nodding, as she vaguely understood but didn't really get it.

"It's kind of an old Irish way of thinking, and it's always bothered me, kind of, even though none of us said anything. It just was that way. I know we've never really sat down to figure out another way, but things are changing. Dad and I moved on and bought that huge ranch down on the Yucatan Peninsula together, and Brad was deeded the ranch, but it's never going to go to a woman, a wife. Trevor is Brad's eldest son, his only son."

"Trevor has autism. How can anything like that go to him?" She couldn't help herself from wondering aloud.

Neil was shaking his head, and she could tell he was wondering, too.

"I don't know, but I'm pretty sure it's something my brother has had to think about. I don't think it was something my grandfather would've ever considered aside from his need to pass it along to a son."

"Can't say I like it, as it's very chauvinistic," Candy said, and Neil laughed.

"Oh, I think Mom would agree with you there, but that's the thing. The more I thought about this resort, which is mine, I realized the land was yours, and then there's our wives, who look to us to support them and look after them." Neil was shaking his head. "I love you, Candy, and I'll look after you, but we're successful because of you just as much as me. I think Andy, Brad, and Jed will agree —they just may need some convincing. Whatever decisions we make should be as a family, and it helps to have our very own legal mind in Diana."

Candy was surprised at Neil for coming up with this. "You think it would work?" she asked.

"I think it would bring us closer together, reunite the family, and…" He looked over at Candy, rubbing her leg. "I'd like to be able to split our time between here and having some fun in the sun."

"You mean we'd still keep this house."

Neil smiled. "Yes."

"And what about Cancun and the estate, the resort? Would we not go back there?"

Neil was still smiling. "Yes, we would, but…" His expression softened. "We'd spend part of the year in Cancun and part of the year here. I want you to feel comfortable, Candy. When you opened up to me last night, telling me about that dream you had, I ached thinking of how sad that must have made you feel. All I can say is I love you so much, and I wouldn't trade our life together for anything. You excite me, you inspire me, and I don't want to do any of this without you by my side. You're irreplaceable. You're Michael and Cat's mother, the one who keeps us together as a family. So what do you say?"

She was stunned. She realized that coming to her and including her was something Neil never would have dreamed of doing when she married him. This man who was her lover, her husband, and her best friend was doing something for the family that would bring them closer together than she could have ever imagined. "Well, I think you should call your brothers and Andy and tell them about this new plan, because I think this is a great idea, Neil."

He leaned forward, sliding his hands over her legs and leaning over her as he kissed her. Pulling back, he breathed deeply. "I already did," he said, smiling brightly.

"And what if I'd said no, then what would you have done?" she teased.

This time he appeared worried. "Would you have considered saying no?"

It was infuriating at times how well he could read her. "No, I wouldn't have." She sighed, and this time when he leaned over her, looking down on her, touching his nose to hers, his lips to hers, he studied her for a minute so deeply.

"With you by my side to keep my head on straight…" He paused for a second as if memorizing everything about her. "You ground me, Candy. You're my voice of reason, and it's because of you that I can do this." Then he kissed her again so tenderly.

CHAPTER 21

There were cars and trucks and other vehicles parked out front of Brad's. The kids were playing outside when Neil pulled in and parked, Cat and Michael in back. He could see the front door opening and Emily waving.

"It looks like everyone's here. Are you ready?" Candy asked, looking happier and far more relaxed than she had in a long time.

He pushed his door open. "Let's go," he said, then watched as his wife lifted out Cat, who raced to her cousins, and then Michael. She swung his diaper bag over her shoulder and carried their dark-haired boy.

It had been a week since Candy had been thrown, a week of putting together plans and ideas and talking with Jed, Brad, and Andy. At the same time, Neil had opened up his heart and told them he couldn't do this without them. He'd worried that they would turn him down, but after a few discussions, talks, emails, and phone calls, Jed, Brad, and Andy had decided to join together with Neil in his resort. They all agreed this resort would be theirs, would belong to the family. It would be security for their wives and children. It would be their place, where they would always come together.

"Neil."

He turned around, surprised to see his mom with her short gray hair. She was dressed so neat and tidy in blues and greens. "Mom, didn't know you were coming," Neil said, and he didn't miss the look Candy cast him from the porch, where she was talking with Diana, who waved and smiled. He leaned down and hugged his mom, giving her a kiss on the cheek.

She reached up and patted his face. "I see you've returned to the handsome, brilliant, clean-cut Neil you'd stashed somewhere for more than a year."

"He was always there," he teased.

"Brad called, told your father and me of your plans for you boys. It made us proud that you're including your brothers and Andy and your wives."

"Well, I kind of got myself in a financial mess, Mom, and I had no one else to blame but myself." He lifted out his computer from the back of the SUV and closed the glass. What Brad, Jed, and Andy had put in for their shares had given Neil the cash he needed, and telling the father–son buying duo that they'd missed their chance had been a relief.

"So does this mean you, Candy, and the kids are coming back to Cancun?" Becky said.

He took in his mom, seeing her flaws and at the same time seeing his mother for the woman she was: a kind, generous, good, loving person who supported her daughter-in-laws and loved her boys and her grandkids. He realized that whatever had happened in her past was just that, her past. It wasn't her future, and it may have shaped her into being who she was today, a role model. He couldn't imagine any better for his children.

"As much as I'd like to, I can't do that to Candy," he said, looking over at his wife, who was smiling and laughing at something Diana had said and was then pulled into the house by Laura, who seemed happier than he'd ever seen her, too. "No, you see, it just took me a while to figure out how to have this resort and give Candy her happily ever after, too. Her family's here. Even though you and Dad are in Cancun and she'll admit she misses the water, sun, warm weather, and her beach, she's happier here than I've ever seen her."

Maybe his mom understood, as her expression for him was something he'd never seen before. "You, your brothers, even that fine nephew of mine are such upstanding men. You make me proud, Neil, doing this for your family, your wife. Putting everything aside to create something truly spectacular that brings people together instead of tearing them apart, that's what makes a man truly amazing. You make me proud, Neil."

He didn't know what to say. He was humbled.

She slid her hand to his arm. "Let's go on in so you can get started on explaining to everyone what they've just gotten themselves into."

Neil laughed as he walked with his mom into the house, giving Diana, Jed, Andy, and Laura a hug and the kids a toss. Neil couldn't remember a time that he'd been happier or more excited than he was now. He listened to the chatter as he set up his PowerPoint presentation and took a look at the women gathered around, watching him, sitting together as one on the sofa. Jed, Brad, and Andy were standing behind them, and his dad was sitting with his mom on the loveseat. The women were chatting again when Neil said, "Okay, I want to welcome everyone to the first ever board meeting of the Friessen family resort." He clicked the mouse, bringing up a picture of his house in

Hoquiam with a sign that said, "Welcome to the head office of *Villa Friessen*."

When he looked over at the shocked expressions on everyone's faces, it was Candy and her sweet smile that reached out to him. She pushed herself off the sofa and threw her arms around his neck. "Thank you," she said as she pressed into him, and she kissed him deeply in front of his family, his parents. Everyone was clapping.

CHAPTER 22

THE RESORT

The weather was hot. Seriously, it was ridiculous. The temperature soared as soon as the double doors at the Cancun airport opened, slamming the scorching humidity into her so much that she had to suck in a breath. For a second or two, she felt as though her body was suffering culture shock. Then she felt sticky and wet and longed for a shower. She was tired and stiff, considering the hours they'd travelled today.

"Candy, just hang back a second," Neil called out as he pushed a luggage cart weighed down with their bag as well as Cat and little Becky, Brad's youngest, perched on top.

Brad was holding Emily's hand as they strode out the doors next, followed by Trevor carrying a duffle bag over his shoulder and wiping his arm across his forehead. "Phew, it's hot," he said, walking over to Candy, who was holding Michael. The baby was quiet for the moment, resting his head on her shoulder. She rubbed his back and could feel him sweating through his cotton shirt and pants.

"It sure is, Trevor. Bet you can't wait to get in the swimming pool." She smiled down at Brad's eldest. She had to remind herself at times that he had autism, because he was so good with everyone. He had a good sense of humor and a good personality and was so fun to be around.

"Yeah" was all he said as Katy came up behind him wearing purple sunglasses, her blond hair tied back in a ponytail.

"Dad said there's supposed to be a car coming for us," she said.

"Oh, man, was that something, coming through customs this time?" Diana said from behind them. "They fingerprinted Jed. You should have seen his face." Her red hair was a mess, probably like all of them, from the hours spent on the plane. "Danny, stay here. You hold my hand. The cars here aren't going to stop," she called out to her little boy, who had her hair color and his father's features. She was also holding Christopher's hand. He was her youngest, who had dark hair like Jed and her eyes. She was wearing a loose top over jeans.

People pushed and filed out of the airport. Locals held up signs for tour buses and tour companies, and crowds of tourists everywhere were looking for taxis to get them to their hotels.

"You haven't said too much. Are you excited, being back?" Diana asked just as Emily slid her arm around Candy's shoulder.

"I swear I'm going to change into my bathing suit and jump in the pool as soon as we get to the house. Rodney and Becky will probably have food ready, too. I'm starved. Couldn't make myself eat any of that airline food," Emily said.

Diana looked between them.

"What?" Emily said.

"Diana was just asking me if I'm happy to be back

here. Honestly, I forgot how hot it was after complaining about the cold back home. I was wishing for this warmth here and the ocean, to have time to walk the beach."

Both women were watching her as if she hadn't really answered them, and she hadn't, come to think of it. She was doing her best to push away the worry lurking in the back of her mind about coming back to Cancun.

"It's fine. It'll be fun," she said, but Diana and Emily exchanged a look that said they didn't quite believe her. "Stop worrying. Let's just see it as the holiday everyone is talking about. It's just a few weeks so everyone can get the resort settled, and all the business matters Neil has been working on." She was going to gesture toward him, but she couldn't move her hand from where it was nestled under Michael's bottom as she held him against her.

"You kids stay here with your mom," Brad said to Trevor and Katy as he took in Emily, Diana, and Candy. He was sweating in the plaid shirt he was wearing. His dark hair was freshly cut, with more gray showing at the sides. He was handsome, with lines around his eyes from the sun and elements, as he spent his days outdoors. He gestured behind them as Neil and Jed came up, both pushing carts filled with luggage.

"What about Andy and Laura?" Jed asked.

"Let's give them a few minutes. They may have gotten held up in customs, too," Jed said. Diana was right: He didn't sound happy.

"Mr. Friessen, over here!" A short, dark-haired Mexican waved from the curb, holding a sign. There was a black limo and a black town car behind it.

"That has to be from the resort," Neil said. "Let's start getting loaded up. I'm sure Andy and Laura should be here by the time we're done. You okay?" Neil was looking right at Candy, and he kept his one hand on the cart where the girls were sitting and his other on Candy's back, sliding down lower to her bottom.

"Yeah, just…" What could she say? From the moment the plane landed, her stomach had been twisted in knots. Stepping off the plane, for some reason she couldn't explain, she felt as if the wall of protection she'd had in the Pacific Northwest was crumbling. Being vulnerable and exposed was something she had been familiar with in the past but didn't expect to feel again.

He waited so patiently for her to answer, not pushing, and she needed to trust him, to tell him, knowing this Neil would listen to her.

"It's going to be okay," he said, glancing back at Cat and Becky, who were giggling as their aunt Diana leaned in, sharing something with them.

"I know it is. It's just I can't help feeling this…"

"Candy, is that you?"

It was a man whose voice she hadn't heard in a long time: Jim Miller, the pediatrician who had helped Cat when Candy first discovered her in the orphanage, the man who had offered her more than friendship. She felt Neil stiffen as Jim, his sun-bleached hair short, his body tall and solid, like her husband's, pulled off sunglasses and showed her a dimpled smile. His blue eyes were far different than Neil's. The way he looked at her was so intense that it could have been just the two of them there, but she could feel everyone's eyes on them, watching them and wondering who this very attractive man was.

"Jim, it's good to see you," Candy said. She didn't miss the shocked expressions on Diana and Emily's faces. Jed was hovering, and Brad had reappeared, extending his hand to Jim.

"Brad Friessen," he said.

Jim shook his hand. "Jim Miller, local pediatrician. I

can see the family resemblance. Didn't know you were back. And is this little miss Cat over here?" Jim not only didn't walk away, he moved over to Cat, who was smiling and giggling. "I guess I don't need to ask how the surgery went. She looks great."

"She does. She's doing fantastic, too," Neil said before Candy could say another word. Neil allowed his hand to fall away from Candy as he reached for Cat and lifted her into his arms. Then he stepped back and slipped his arm around her and Michael. She considered—how could she not?—that he was making a point.

Even Jed appeared to wonder as he glanced over to Brad. Diana mouthed, "Who is this?" But now was not the time, as everything was coming back, much like a sucker punch: Maria, Jim, and that feeling of being on the outside, looking in—but she had her family now and reinforcements in Emily and Brad, she reminded herself again.

"Jim, you still have a practice here?" She had never been good at small talk, but she didn't want to answer any questions.

Jim took in Brad and Jed, but he didn't look Neil's way before glancing down at Candy. "I do. Heard you moved up north. Are you back or visiting?"

By the way he took in Michael, she wondered whether he knew who he was, the baby from the surrogate who had almost ended what she had with Neil. Jim didn't say anything else, though, and he gave her a stiff smile before she could answer. "Good to see you, Candy, Neil." Then he stepped away, leaving her with her family and a lot of curious questions she wasn't too interested in answering right now.

"Hey, is the car here?" Andy called out from where he pushed a luggage cart stacked with bags, the twins on top, Gabriel helping by holding one of the bars on the cart.

Laura, with her hair pulled up in a messy bun beside him, wore a big smile as she held their baby, Sarah, who was cooing and kicking her bare legs, wearing just a diaper and a cotton shirt.

The odd look Neil gave her had Candy looking away, starting for one of the two cars, and climbing in.

CHAPTER 23

Neil didn't bother drying off from the pool after climbing out. Even as the sun dropped lower, it was still warm. He had missed this heat, this comfort, and the estate, this massive property he still owned with his father and the ranch at the north end, where there were a herd of Angus his father had raised. Ranching was in his father's blood, in Brad's and Jed's and in Andy's, he supposed, but it had never been something that drove him.

He glanced over to the kids splashing in the pool, Candy, Emily, Diana, and Laura at one end, laughing and chatting. They were having a lot of fun catching up, and he was happy that Candy was fitting in. All the women were grower closer in their tight-knit family.

"Come on, baby, let's get you dried off," Andy said as he stepped out of the pool, wearing dark swim trunks, carrying Sarah, who was wearing a cute little pink bikini over a water diaper. The twins were in two life jackets, playing with the other kids in the pool with air mattresses and floaties.

Neil rested in one of the five lounge chairs that had been set out around the pool. The umbrella was closed beside him, and he considered opening it for a second but changed his mind, wanting what was left of the late afternoon sun.

Andy took the lounge chair beside him, glancing over to Candy and back to him. "Mind telling me what that was we walked into at the airport? Who was the guy talking with you? I saw how you were."

Neil didn't think Andy had heard, as he and Laura had been the last to come out from customs—with customs officers, this time, who'd been unusually diligent. He shrugged and glanced over to where Brad and Jed were also in the pool, playing with the kids.

"Jed mentioned something was going on," Andy said.

Neil wished he had a stiff drink right now as he thought of Jim Miller. The man had been in love with Candy, and Neil could tell he still was. "A local doctor. Met him when Candy found Cat in the orphanage. He's the one responsible for helping get Cat her cochlear implant so she could hear. He diagnosed her."

Andy was smiling at Sarah, the beautiful baby perched on his knee, sitting up and now about six months old. "Can tell when something has you twisted all up. So what's the deal between him and your wife, a problem?" Andy asked.

"Pride, I guess you can say. When I almost destroyed what Candy and I had because of my obsession, he was there. He saw everything I did to screw it up, to hurt Candy. He became her shoulder to cry on."

The expression on Andy's face appeared questioning, and Neil wasn't sure whether it was about the situation, about Jim, or about why Neil was sitting back and doing nothing. Neil was wondering what to do, too, considering

Candy hadn't said a word about their run in with Jim. "If Candy were ever to leave me, I feared it would be for him," he said.

Andy just watched him in that dark, brooding way he had when someone was doing something not quite right. "I see."

"Yeah," Neil said, because neither did he have a clue what he was going to do. It was a problem, but at the same time it wasn't. This worry about the situation was something that could be a problem if he let it, though.

"Well, well, well, if it isn't the dashing, charming Friessen men!" Stella, his redheaded banker, appeared from the back door of the house. His dad, dressed in light shorts and a striped tennis shirt, was beside her. Stella was wearing pumps, a red skirt, and a white sleeveless blouse. Her face was caked with a heavy coating of makeup, and her short curled hair was tied back with a scarf that dangled down her back.

"Stella!" he said. It was good to see her. He hadn't realized how much he'd missed her as a friend and business advisor. There was something about dealing with a banker who understood what he created and did. There was also the fact that he'd made her a lot of money.

She lifted her hand and waved to Candy, who waved back. "Look at all of you. You have quite the collection of family here."

Neil reached for a folded white towel on the foot of his lounge chair and stood up, reaching out his hand to Stella.

"Oh, stop that," she said. "Come here and give me a hug." She went to hug him, her hands on his arms, and made a face. "Or not! You're all wet." She gestured to the pool and stepped around him. "Candy, all of you, come on out of the pool. I want to have a talk with you regarding your little venture." She had a way of stepping in and taking charge.

"I thought we were going to meet in the morning," Neil said. Of course, right now, he was starting to wonder what was going on.

"Things change, and important issues come up," Stella replied.

Neil watched as his brothers waded out of the pool. Diana was in her blue one-piece bathing suit, Candy in her black bikini, Emily in a peach and green two piece that covered her to her belly button, and Laura in a ruffled pink number that showed her fantastic body. Neil looked to his dad, who said something to his mom, who had come out carrying Michael. He was rubbing his eyes, probably having just woken up.

"We were just getting to that," Rodney said. He called out to the kids in the pool and then said, "Anna and your mother will take the kids in and get them dried off while we have our meeting. Dinner will be soon, too."

"Becky, you need any help?" Emily called out.

Becky just gestured toward them. "No, you have some things to discuss. We'll be just fine looking after the kids."

Chairs were pulled around, scraping on the concrete.

"Neil, I called Stella," Rodney said, and that had him doing a double take. Andy was still holding Sarah, and Anna, the housekeeper, leaned down and asked to take her. Neil only caught bits and pieces of what everyone was saying, but something in his dad's voice made him realize there was a reason for this early visit.

"Was having lunch at your resort with friends, and there was a problem."

He couldn't imagine what that would be. Having been away and out of the daily running of everything, he felt at a complete loss. It was a feeling he didn't like. "Oh, and what was that?"

Stella turned from hugging Candy and said, "Neil, those buyers you had lined up, the Pirez father and son? Well, hate to tell you this, but they screwed you."

CHAPTER 24

C andy was sharing a lounger with Diana, Emily was joining Brad, and Laura was still wrapping a towel around herself. Candy scooted to the middle, making room for her to sit. Neil was just staring at Stella in shock as if he couldn't figure out what to say. His hair was getting long again, and the wet ends brushed his ears, curling in waves.

He seemed to pull himself together then, and he fingered his hair back and rubbed his hand over the back of his head the way he did when he was thinking. "Wait, start at the beginning. What happened?"

She'd only seen Neil like this a few times, all business, and he hadn't cast one glance her way or to anyone else. It was as if he was absorbing all of it, handling all of it.

"Your dad called me before you got in. He was down at your resort, having lunch, and…"

"Stella, I'll tell the rest." Rodney rested his hand on her shoulder.

"By all means," Stella said.

"I was with Bill and Larry for lunch at the resort. We stop there weekly, but this week we waited, ordered drinks.

Our meal seemed to be taking a really long time. When I went over and asked the waiter what was up after noticing that the staff seemed unusually distressed, I found out that your chef and sous chef had walked out before lunch, so I went looking for the manager. He tried to assure me all was well until I said who I was, your father. Then he pulled me aside and informed me the Pirezes had left and had taken their chefs with them. I didn't realize how much worse things were until I called Stella."

Candy couldn't believe this, and she listened to Jed swear. Brad was pretty quiet as he watched Neil, waiting maybe to see what he said. Andy, too, appeared to be thinking some pretty heavy thoughts.

"This doesn't sound good," Diana whispered beside her.

"I made some calls after hearing from Rodney," Stella said, "and it appears the Pirezes also pulled their general manager, who, as you know, Neil, came with them when they were considering buying."

"So basically what you're saying is that right now, no one is running my resort," Neil finally said. Candy's heart ached as she thought of his dream being flushed down the toilet.

"You had some good staff already in place, so your assistant manager was called in and has brought in some emergency staff in the meantime, but that's only until you all here can figure out your next step. As I see it, everything you planned has been undone."

"What about the money that was deposited?" Neil said. Candy didn't miss the edge in his voice, and maybe Stella already knew, as she reached a hand out, her long nails painted the same vibrant red they always were.

"That would have been a big red flag at my end. It's all there, but you're going to have to do an internal audit, find out what's still missing, because what I can tell you is that nothing has been deposited in the company account in eight days."

"Okay, I'm going to get dressed." Neil slung a towel over his shoulder Andy stood up and slipped around Rodney. "Laura, I'm going to go in with Neil."

"You should take Diana, too," Laura said.

Candy wondered what Jed thought, as he seemed tense, as if he had other ideas about where his wife should be. Candy looked over to Diana, who seemed uncertain.

Neil finally turned, taking in all of them. She knew he blamed himself for what was happening. "Diana, yes, please come," he said. "We could use your legal mind, considering I don't know what we're going to find."

"Just let me get dressed." She squeezed Candy's hand.

As Candy stood up to go to Neil, he turned away and walked into the house, so she sat back down beside Laura. When she glanced up, she noticed Brad's gaze heavy on her. He seemed to be thinking and then said to her, "There's one thing about my brother that I do know right now. He's probably kicking himself in the ass for this."

"Maybe so, Brad, but it is what it is," Rodney said. "Can't change it, can only fix it. Let's get the kids fed and then find out where we go from here." Rodney then said something to Stella that Candy couldn't make out.

"I'm going to go change Sarah and then change into some dry clothes myself," Laura said before excusing herself. Emily followed.

"Yeah, fun's over," Brad said. "Come on, Jed. Let's get changed."

Stella stepped around him, patting his arm, and stopped in front of Candy. She realized everyone was going into the house, leaving her and Stella alone.

"It's good to see you, Stella," Candy said as Stella

scooted up a chair and sat down, crossing her slim tanned legs. For a woman in her seventies, she really brought sexy back. Candy hoped she would look as good as Stella did at her age.

"Things good between you and that hunk of a man you have?" Stella smiled.

"Yeah, we're happy," she said—except she still needed to talk to Neil about seeing Jim at the airport. She'd been rattled, and she knew he was irritated.

"Good, you deserve it. You both do. Was worried there, but glad you stuck it out. If any two deserved each other, you two did. I knew it, he knew it. Marriage is hard work, but he all but gave everything away for you. That's real love." She gestured in the direction of the resort, and Candy wondered whether Stella was trying to make her feel bad. Right now, she was questioning everything and wondering whether she was the selfish one, pushing Neil so hard to move away from here just so she could have peace of mind.

"Oh, I can see you questioning your decisions. You never have been good at hiding things, Candy. It's not always a good thing. You need to add a little mystery to yourself. Don't let everyone know what you're thinking."

"Well, it's because of me that Neil decided to sell. Did you see how he left? He didn't say a word to me. I thought we were past this. He's angry. Maybe he does blame me."

Stella waved in the air between them. "Oh, don't read too much into that. He's just a man who's angry, disillusioned, and had the rug yanked out from under him. Men don't always handle things so well. He trusted this father–son team, and maybe he should have kept a closer eye on things, but this isn't on you. A lot of things brought you here, and it may not be that bad, anyway. Look on the bright side."

"Oh, and what would that be?" she wondered aloud as she listened to the voices drifting from the house.

"Your family, this big family, all of you are now part of this big dream of Neil's. It's not just Neil alone becoming king of the world. There's all of you." She gestured to Candy and over to the house. "This legacy you're creating of a family-run resort, well, I for one happen to think it's a fabulous idea. It'll bring you closer." She patted Candy's leg. "And just one more thing."

She looked up as Stella stood and smoothed down her skirt, then pulled her sunglasses down so Candy could see her bold blue eyes, the smoky lids and the lashes with a coating of mascara.

"You need to stand your ground with Neil," Stella said. "Pull on those big-girl pants, and when he gets back, upset and all, which he will be, you make him talk to you."

As she watched Stella, whose heels clicked on the cement patio, Candy sat alone around the pool. She wondered whether Stella had any idea that with Neil, that was easier said than done.

Candy was slicing through a piece of steak and scooping it up with beans, salsa, and rice.

"So have you heard from Neil?" Emily pulled up a chair beside her at the patio table where she sat alone. She could see Becky inside with the kids. Anna was helping, and Jed was carrying one of the boys and sitting him at the table in the dining room.

"No," she said as she chewed, and Emily gave her a well-meaning look.

"Candy, do you want to talk about what's going through your head? Both Brad and I noticed the way Neil left."

"You mean how upset he was? He barely looked my way and left without a word to me, his wife." She cut another piece of meat, but she had lost her appetite, sitting here worrying and wondering about what had happened at Neil's multimillion-dollar resort, the one he'd dreamed of but had walked away from for her. Now they were almost broke, and he had brought in his brothers and Andy to partner with him in a dream that could end up being such a mess it might come between all of them. Money had a way of doing that.

"Yeah, that." Emily reached over and touched Candy's hand.

Candy leaned back, sighing as she took in Laura, who was coming their way, carrying her six-month-old baby in one arm and a plate in the other. She was dressed in a light sundress with spaghetti straps, her hair hanging loose.

"Was wondering where you went to. Brad is inside on the phone with Andy." Laura set her plate down, and Candy couldn't help reaching for the baby.

"Give her to me while you eat," she said. Sarah was such an easy baby, content and happy, and she sat perched on Candy's lap and smiled so brightly.

"Did he say what was going on?" Emily asked. Candy just sat back and listened.

"Andy told me before I put Brad on that they have a pile of books to go through, but it was quite a mess. The comptroller with signing authority was nowhere to be found. Andy's good at the business side of things and books, and at times I feel really stupid around him, but at least he's sharing with me now." She winced, looking up at Emily, her cheeks flushing a bit. "I never finished high school. I had to drop out, and at times like this I don't know what I can contribute."

"Hey, it's got nothing to do with education," Candy said. "We're family. This is what Neil wanted, for all of us to be part of this, and our kids." At least Andy was calling Laura and filling her in, though. At one time, Candy knew that hadn't been something Andy did. Neil...he should have called. It hurt to think he was leaving her out.

"I told Andy I want to go back to school, to graduate at least. It's easier now since I can do it all online."

It was really nice seeing this part of Laura, Candy thought.

"Good for you!" Emily said. "You should do it. I hope you do, even if you don't do anything with it. It's about knowing that you can do what you set your mind to. Andy isn't opposed, is he?" Emily frowned, maybe thinking the same thing Candy was: The Friessen men liked their women at home.

Laura was shaking her head, chewing. She wiped her mouth with her napkin. "No, Andy has been my biggest supporter. He's encouraged me. He even pulled all the information and the registration to get me started. I love him so much for this." She smiled. "At times, with him behind me, I honestly believe I can do anything."

Candy couldn't help smiling. Seeing this confidence in Laura that she hadn't before, it was as if she was growing up around them. Maybe she'd been too critical of Andy. He was a mystery, but anyone could see how much his family meant to him. He was a fool in love with Laura, the kind of love that snuck in, creeping up on people. It was inspiring.

"What?" Laura looked up, and her cheeks took on a hint of pink again, maybe from the way Emily and Candy were watching her.

"I'm so happy for you, Laura, and seeing you and Andy together and so in love," Emily added. "It's wonderful. Speaking of wonderful…at the airport today, Candy, who was that man who didn't try to hide his interest in you? Haven't seen that side of Neil in a long time. He was absolutely territorial." Emily was watching her.

Laura froze with a forkful of food halfway to her mouth. "Huh?"

"He was the pediatrician who helped me with Cat," Candy said. She wasn't sure what else to say and couldn't remember what she'd shared with Emily. Laura was completely in the dark, but then, she and Andy had just come out of the airport when Jim was leaving. Candy hadn't shared many confidences with anyone other than Brad and Emily. Of course, that didn't seem to satisfy Emily, so Candy just shrugged. "He was a friend to me when Neil was stuck on the surrogate, moving her in, when we got so far down that road that I thought it might be over. Jim was a friend."

Laura was even watching her now with something resembling worry, concern. For a minute, Candy thought she may have been suspecting there had been something more.

"It was nothing more than that. He offered me his spare room."

Emily's eyes softened.

"He fought with Neil," she said, and this time Laura stopped chewing, her cheeks puffed out, her eyes wide. "I never knew until recently that Jim had shown up here and hit Neil. It was him who was the catalyst for Neil to come after me. He told Neil he loved me." She smiled at the horror in Laura's eyes. Emily rubbed her brow and reached over to touch Candy's arm.

"Oh, Candy, I can see why Neil was the way he was. That's awkward."

"Andy would have killed him," Laura added and then shrugged. "If it was me."

"He's a handsome man, Candy," Emily said. Candy hoped she wasn't about to ask her how she felt about Jim.

"Yes, he is, but I think you'd both agree with me that we can't choose who we fall in love with. It wouldn't have mattered with Jim, because I love Neil. I always have, I always will."

"Candy, it'll be all right. Just have a talk with Neil when

he gets back, put his mind at ease. He loves you, and he knows you love him." Emily leaned back just as Brad called out from the doorway. "Excuse me. It looks like I need to go give Brad a hand with the kids."

Candy gazed down at Sarah, who was sitting so quietly, cooing and happy. When she glanced up, from the way Laura was watching her, she wondered whether she'd shared too much.

CHAPTER 26

The records were shredded. He still couldn't believe it when he walked back into the top-floor office beside the penthouse suite, which overlooked the pools and one of the four restaurants below.

"So there are no accounting records for six months is what you're saying," Andy said.

Neil had finally tracked down the department heads, sat each of them down at an emergency meeting, and established an agenda, prioritizing what needed to be done to keep the resort up and running, employees working, and guests happy.

"Did you hear me, Neil?" Andy asked as he lowered himself into a dark blue cloth chair across from the massive oak desk Neil was sitting behind. Windows filled one wall, and he could look out at the ocean and the miles of sandy beach. He could see the dock that led out to the outlook where the health club did yoga every morning, and the ferry to the island was passing by. This part of Cancun was away from the other hotels and resorts, with a private sandy beach for guests.

"Neil?" Andy said again, and Neil finally looked over just as Diana, his gorgeous sister-in-law, strode in dressed so casually in a light green cotton skirt, a white T-shirt, and flip flops. She had a pen stuck behind her ear and glasses on, and she was reading something as she sat in the other chair beside Andy. She looked first to Neil and then him as if she had just realized something.

"Everything all right?" she asked.

Neil picked up a pen that had been tossed on the desk on top of the scattered papers he'd gone through while trying to figure out what was going on. "Andy was saying that all the financial records for the past six months regarding income have been shredded. They've also been purged from the computer system, as the payroll clerk I just finished speaking with pointed out to me."

"So we don't know what kind of money came in, what these guys walked out with," Diana said.

Neil was shaking his head. These men were smart enough not to have left a paper trail. Maybe this was their way of getting back at Neil for taking away their opportunity, but then they'd dragged their feet for too long, anyway. It was time to take the resort back. They had made their position clear.

He gestured to Diana, who pulled her glasses off and stuck them on top of her head. She glanced to Andy, who was leaning there casually, wearing a plain blue T-shirt and blue jeans, sandals on his feet. It wasn't his brothers but Andy, with his head for business, his shrewdness, that Neil needed right now.

"I'm feeling as if I've gotten all of you into something that could end up taking us down a rabbit hole. This is…" He stopped. His brothers and Andy had pitched in a sizable chunk of cash to bail him out. This had been his business plan, his idea to bring the family together and work together with his brothers to create something bigger and better.

"Stop it right now. Seriously, Neil, we're in this together, and right now things could be worse, way worse."

"Andy's right, Neil. From what I can see, you still have an operating resort, minus a lot of cash. The only problem may be creditors who haven't been paid."

"And, apparently, a missing head chef and sous chef putting excess work on the remaining staff," Neil said. He leaned forward at his desk, taking in Andy, a very capable businessman, and Diana, his brother's wife, a stay-at-home mom with a license to practice law. He was so glad they were here. "I've already met with the head of food and beverage, and he's now working with the kitchen staff. The problem is that they need direction, but all isn't lost. We've borrowed a chef from one of the other resorts. The manager owes me a favor, so I'm collecting. He'll be here tomorrow, and then after that…we replace who we need to and take over, putting this world-class resort back on the map."

"Sounds like a plan." Diana smiled, wiping her forehead, appearing tired, but then, it was late, nearly eleven. The kids would be asleep, and he could imagine his brother would be pacing.

"What do you say we come back to it in the morning, fill everyone in, and see if we can't get started?"

IT WAS dark when they pulled into the estate. The lights were on, glowing from the windows. The front door opened, and there was Jed, standing and waiting. Diana climbed out and went right into his arms.

Brad had turned in already, and so had his parents. All

seemed quiet. Neil said goodnight to Andy at the top of the stairs as he turned right down the hallway to his parents' wing. He stopped in the doorway of the room across from his, taking in the kids sleeping. Michael was in his crib, Cat and Becky sharing the queen bed.

He expected Candy to be asleep as he opened the door, but she looked up from where she was sitting up in bed, reading. She had on a peach nightgown with spaghetti straps. Her knees up, she was a picture. He closed the door just as she closed her book.

"Everything okay?" she asked, and there was a moment when it seemed the wall that had been there between them before was slipping back up. He didn't like it.

"Could be better, but wasn't as bad as it could have been. But then, we won't know more until we really get into the books, the numbers, and all the nitty gritty." He was out of the loop and starting from scratch, which put him at a huge disadvantage. Tomorrow he'd have to make some calls, start schmoozing, and give the staff some breathing room until they could have everything in order.

Neil was sitting on the bed, unbuttoning his shirt. He kicked off his shoes and then realized Candy hadn't said anything. He slid around and could see she was thinking as she pulled her lower lip between her teeth.

"What's going on?" he asked. The last thing he wanted was Candy pulling away to write everything down in that damn journal again. After how hard he tried, at times, it was beginning to feel as if he were walking on eggshells. He didn't want to go back to that. He couldn't go back to that.

"Did I push you to this, with me needing to be away from here? Tell me, Neil, did I?"

"I was distracted, Candy. The fact is I put more trust in

the Pirezes than I should have. I should have followed up. I still owned this resort even though the sale was in the works. It comes back on me, not you." Even saying it the way he did didn't comfort Candy, he could tell, but then, he wasn't entirely sure she wasn't right in some way. "Look, I'm tired. Let's just get some sleep." He pulled off his shirt and started in to the large walk-in closet where all their clothes had been put away.

"So is this what I'm in for, being back here in Cancun, the old Neil who kept everything from me and expected me to just do as I was told?"

He stepped out and took in the fire in his wife's expression. She was angry now, her arms crossed, maybe looking for a fight. "No, I'm tired, Candy. What is it you want to know, that this is entirely on me, the way my resort is teetering on the brink of disaster? That I dropped the ball, that I screwed up with my obsession, that it came between us and you were already two feet out the door, walking away from me? There was no choice between you and this resort, because it wasn't a choice. There was no compromise, not really," he added when she went to say something.

"Why don't you just say what this is really about, Neil?" Candy threw back the covers and slipped from bed but stopped just out of arm's reach as if she needed to have distance between them.

"Oh, don't you dare go there."

"Why not, Neil? Ever since we ran into Jim Miller at the airport, with your reaction to him, I've been getting the cold shoulder from you as if you blame me for some part of that," she said, gesturing and getting louder.

He ran his hand over his head, maybe to try to dial it back, but she was touching on that one thing, the image he didn't want in his head. It infuriated him to think that man was still waiting in the wings for his wife. "He's in love with you still," Neil said.

She was still standing there as if considering what to say. "Love is a two-way street, Neil, and I don't love him. He was my friend. I love you."

"He's waiting for you. I didn't realize, or maybe I did, that he would be right there for you in a second, trying to win you over."

"You must have very little respect for me to think I could be wooed and swayed like that. I'm with you, not him." She still hadn't moved.

"But what would it have taken, Candy, for him to win you over, to get your attention, to get you to consider him?" He stepped closer to her, and he didn't like the expression that came over her. She seemed to be digging in but conflicted, not a good sign. His heart sank.

He reached for her and pulled her against him, jamming his hands in her hair, holding her so she couldn't move. He just looked at her, breathing hard, wanting to mark her so everyone knew she was his and backed the hell off. He leaned in, taking her lips, kissing rough, bruising, claiming, and tasting her, making it clear he wasn't going to stand for any man to think he could step in and make sweet eyes at his wife. Maybe he needed to make it clear to Candy, to embed the understanding inside her so she knew deep to her bones, her soul, that he owned her.

He ran his hand down her back, over her bottom, feeling her softness as he walked her back to the bed. He wasn't thinking, he couldn't think, as he was taking her, and maybe she understood his need or realized there was no point in pushing him back. He pulled at her nighty and ripped it down the middle. She gasped, but he didn't give her a moment to think about it as he pushed the sides open, showing her plump, magnificent breasts that had never nursed a child. His hands ran down and skimmed over the part of her that would only be touched by him. He'd be dammed if another man ever had the chance. He reached down, undid his zipper, and pushed into her hard and deep, maybe to drive home the point that this was his: her body, her soul. He didn't speak. He touched, he moved, he tasted as he took what he knew deep down would only be his.

He would kill Jim Miller and dump his body somewhere it would never be found if he ever came sniffing around his wife again.

CHAPTER 27

"Are you asleep?"

Neil was lying on top of her, still inside her. "Hmm," he grunted. Maybe he couldn't move after what had happened. It hadn't been making love. That wasn't what Neil had done. For the first time, she felt as if she'd been unable to say a word while he'd taken her, believing she belonged to him body, mind, and soul. It had been over the top for Neil, but she'd felt his urgency as if he needed to make a point, maybe for him, for his need. Men never behaved this way if they didn't care.

Maybe that was why she was giving in. She lay there as if needing to let him have this.

He still didn't move as he breathed deeply again, but she knew he was awake as she could feel him thinking. With Neil, it wasn't so much him saying anything. It was the way his body moved and relaxed, the tension that was very much still in him.

"Is this your way of punishing me, or is it something else?" she asked as she kept her arms around his back, holding him.

He pulled away and glanced down at her, the lamp shining into the conflict in his face, the emotions he didn't try to hide from her. He reached over and flicked off the light, then sat up and pulled off his pants before lying on his back beside her, sighing again as if he couldn't, wouldn't, speak.

So she rolled to her side, the ripped gown catching her shoulder. She sat up and pulled it off, tossing it over the side of the bed.

"Was I too rough?"

She could hear something in his voice that worried her, so she lay down again on her side, touching him, allowing her foot to trail up, feeling the hair, the muscles on his long legs, legs she loved getting caught up with hers. She rested her head on his chest, and she was glad when he pressed his hand to her back and held her there. His touch again seemed almost desperate.

"Maybe I like rough, Neil. It was surprising, is all. I don't think you'd have let me up, would you have?"

He didn't answer at first as he continued to rub her back. "He can't ever have you, Candy. You know that, right?"

The way he said it, she had to shut her eyes just to ground herself, because there was an edge there. She knew Jim Miller was Neil's Achilles' heel. Everything about the man would drive him to be unreasonable. If she hadn't understood that before, it was clear now more than ever. Every man had something that could push him over the edge or make him do something unreasonable, something dangerous, and that knowledge could never be entrusted to anyone else.

"I know." She sighed and allowed her hand to trace circles over his chest. Then he gripped her hand, brought it to his mouth, and kissed it. "I just never realized how far over the edge he pushed you. I'd never cheat, Neil. He's not for me." She said it so softly as he swept his hand over her head. He was so clingy and touchy right now, as if he was trying to reassure himself. "What can I do to make you feel better, to help you understand he has no chance? I gave my heart to you, my love." She rested her chin on his chest, looking up at him in the dark.

He just kept touching her head, her hair, as if burning it all into memory. It was so possessive, and he was being downright territorial. She got that as she worked to calm him back to the reasonable Neil, but all he did was roll her over until he was on top of her again. She could feel him against her, thick and long and ready for her. He didn't kiss her as he entered her slowly, his arms beside her, looking down on her. His breath was warm as he moved again, and she understood that tonight was about feeling and allowing her husband to have her over and over until he was clear, in his mind, that she was his.

CHAPTER 28

"Here's your coffee." Neil held a large green mug to Candy where she was sitting alone in a cushy chair in the light-filled living room. Her eyelids appeared heavy and her body limp. The french doors were open, allowing the air in, and the potted plants his mother loved were in front of the expanse of windows. The fireplace and the mantle above it were the centerpiece, and his eye caught the huge family photo that now hung there. He'd never seen it before, but it was one he recognized of all of them from the anniversary party for his parents. Everyone was in it, all the kids except Sarah, who was the lump in Laura's belly in the photo.

"Your mom had that one blown up," Candy said. "I can see how she loves to look at it and see all of us. She's proud of everyone." She sipped on the coffee, her legs tucked beneath her, and she appeared to want to lay her head on the arm of the chair and go to sleep. "Mmm. Good coffee."

He pulled out the ottoman and sat in front of her, reaching out and putting his hand on her bare legs. She had pulled on white shorts and a brown tank top, and she looked gorgeous. "Didn't let you have much sleep last night. Maybe you want to have a nap. Anna can watch the kids. Katy, last I looked, had Michael attached to her hip and was carrying him around. You didn't stay for our breakfast meeting."

In fact, she'd slipped out when Brad and Jed had asked about the Pirezes' whereabouts and had been deciding on their morning plans. His mom had smiled at Candy as she left, and Brad had leveled Neil with a look as if everyone knew why she was so tired this morning. No one had said anything when she slipped out, even when Neil had hesitated and considered going after her. He hadn't, though, sensing her need for space.

He had been pulled back into the discussion when Jed, for the first time, had deferred to Diana, looking for her ideas. Brad had said he understood the ranching business, but hospitality was a foreign arena, out of his area of expertise. What they all agreed was that the leadership had to come from Neil. Andy had been quiet, only nodding in agreement.

Neil really felt an enormous responsibility for Jed and Brad, for all of them, for the money they had put into something that was his specialty, his niche. They were trusting him.

Candy reached out and touched his arm. "You're bothered about Jim still?"

He shook his head, wanting to apologize for his need for her the night before, for how he hadn't been able to control himself with her. He'd been rough, unable to sleep, and instead of letting Candy rest, he'd pawed at her and spent most of the night inside her over and over—and she'd let him.

"No, my brothers, the family, everyone is looking to me

to figure this out. God, Candy, if I screw this up, it's not just our money, it's my brothers' and Andy's."

"Hey." She leaned forward and set her coffee down on the table beside her. "You listen to me. You're so good at what you do that there isn't a chance Brad, Jed, or Andy would doubt you. So don't you start doubting yourself. Just focus on what you need to do to accomplish the goal, nothing else. Don't listen to anyone. I have faith in you, Neil. Don't stop believing in yourself."

He was so lucky. He wondered how he'd never realized how important Candy was for him, how important it was for him. To hear her tell him how much she believed in him without question felt freeing. Success really wasn't about being rich and wealthy; it was about the support he had behind him, and for him that was Candy. He realized then that this resort would be a success because she was standing behind him, encouraging him.

"You're so good for me," he said, smiling at her and rubbing her leg, her ankle, touching her any way he could.

"I know. You made your point last night." She leaned back and stretched, and now he felt bad for how he'd allowed that wave of emotion to take over his reasoning. It had been his insecurity about her having someone in the wings wanting what he had, threatening his happily ever after.

"Again, I'm sorry. Can't promise it won't happen again, though."

"I know." She sighed in a way that was filled with weariness, satisfaction, and resignation, but all in a good way.

"I love you," he said.

This time she looked at him deeply, as if reaching inside him and finally understanding. She said, "I know you do."

CHAPTER 29

Neil stood in the courtyard, watching the crowd of vacationers staying at his resort. Jed and Andy were speaking with one of the sales reps who was part of the team selling timeshares. It was something the Pirezes had started. He had a pretty good idea of the amount of dollars that had come out of the deals to date, hooking them into a pool of resorts worldwide.

"This is pretty slick, Neil." Brad rested his hand on his shoulder, and this was the first time Neil had seen him dressed in shorts. If his white legs were any indication, Neil was positive it had been a long time.

"Yeah, I forgot how spectacular this place is," Neil said —and it was. One of the pools surrounded one of the outdoor covered restaurants, another had a large bridge with a rope swing, and another held a volleyball net. There was a smaller one off to the side reserved for kids, since adults preferred having a space to swim without little diapered babies bobbing in the water.

The wait staff wandered between the poolside lounge

chairs filled with sunbathers drinking, snacking, and relaxing. That was what a resort was all about.

"We may have to come and enjoy some of these amenities. You really created something high class and high end, very well put together. How's the food here?" Candy asked as she walked up with Emily, Diana, and Laura. They were all dressed smartly, with Laura and Diana opting for sundresses, Diana also wearing a white floppy hat. Emily was wearing shorts and a tank top, just like Candy.

"That's a great question. Was always fantastic before. Franco," Neil called out to the sales rep chatting with Jed and Andy.

"Yes, sir?" he said.

"How's the food in the restaurants?"

"Still good. Many guests enjoy the simplicity and ease of the buffet, especially with fussy kids who aren't eager to sit and wait for a meal to be ordered and cooked. Other guests who are more choosey have complained it lacks flavor, but the Mexican and Italian restaurants and the steakhouse are raved about. They are very good, even with the chef and his assistant leaving."

Neil just nodded. That eased his mind, because nothing could spell disaster more than the food being subpar. People here were on vacation, wanting good food and drinks, comfortable rooms, and lots of activities and fun.

Jed said, "Franco was just saying that the recreation department has activities for everyone running throughout the day—games, sports, cooking lessons, and apparently a tequila tasting at four today."

Neil wondered for a minute why Jed had brought that up.

He shrugged. "Just saying that if I were to take a vacation, I'd like a place that had options, including a club where the kids would have other kids to play with."

"Good point, brother. That was actually one of my ideas right from the beginning. I want this to be a resort people remember and come back to year after year because it provides everything for the entire family."

"This is amazing, Neil," Emily said as she slid her arm around Brad's waist, glancing up at him.

"Mr. Friessen!" Neil heard a woman call his name, and he glanced to where she hurried his way. She wore a dark skirt and a white blouse, with a name-tag pinned above her breast. Her heels clicked on the patio, and her dark hair was pinned up in a very neat bun. She had to be one of the front desk clerks, but he didn't recognize her.

She was out of breath when she drew close enough to speak. "Mr. Friessen, there are some people to see you. I was told by my manager to find you and let you know."

People, what people? "And who is it who's looking for me?" he said. Next on the list was to have a chat with the department heads to make sure they didn't send staff looking for him without all the details. That was sloppy.

"I'm not sure who it is, sir, but my manager said it was important. Mr. Pirez is one of them." She spoke with urgency.

"And where are they?" he asked, feeling a lot of emotion. He was fighting the urge to demand that the man who'd tried to dismantle what he'd built return to him all the documents and the money he'd stolen.

"In your office, sir."

Neil hadn't waited for her to finish before starting across the courtyard to the lobby and the elevator that would take him to the top floor.

CHAPTER 30

Seeing Neil take off as if the devil were on his heels, Candy worried for a minute about how he'd react to Mr. Pirez, who'd basically lied to him and strung him along. But then, Brad, Andy, and Jed were right behind him. Franco was now talking to the young woman who'd rushed out, and both of them seemed a little panicked.

"What should we do?" Emily said, standing beside her.

Candy looked over to Diana, who said, "I think we should tag along. Neil has a good head on his shoulders, but this is personal, and I know with our men, personal can sometimes cloud good business sense."

Laura said nothing as she looked around in awe at the resort, her expression conveying that it was grand, something she couldn't quite get a handle on. But then, who could, on something of this size?

Maybe Candy understood Laura's perspective better than anyone. She fell in beside her, following Diana and Emily as they hurried behind the men, who were already inside and making their way to the elevator.

"You know, my little house was right over there, where

that little sports bar is by the second pool. This was my property at one time. Now look."

"It still is, Candy," Diana said from where she held open the door. "Don't forget, the land is in your name. Neil never changed it."

She wasn't sure whether her expression showed her surprise, considering she'd signed it over to him. It had been her wedding present to him, giving her husband the one thing he'd always wanted: his resort, his dream.

"Oh." She watched as the elevator doors slid closed, the men obviously not waiting for them, which was maybe a good thing.

"I can tell by your expression that you didn't know Neil kept it all in your name. Even the title on the resort complex, the shell corporation, has you listed as an equal shareholder," Diana said as she pushed the up button.

Candy could feel Laura and Emily watching her, staring. Maybe they were as surprised as she was. The fact was she'd just assumed Neil had everything in his name. "I didn't know. I just thought…"

Diana was looking up at the floor numbers displayed on the elevator prompt. "Didn't surprise me, Candy. That man would give everything to you and then some. He loves you so much. When I saw it, it made sense to me." Maybe it was the way she was staring at Diana. Even Emily and Laura appeared confused. As the elevator doors slid open and they all stepped in, Diana said, "Neil is my friend, my brother-in-law, and was always there when Jed and I went through our troubles. He's like all of our men. He'd never, ever take from a woman."

CHAPTER 31

His heart was hammering in his chest as he beat a path, his feet pounding the ground as he rounded the corner of the hall toward the office beside the penthouse on the top floor. He pushed open the glass door and saw two people standing at the window, looking out. He barely glanced behind him to Jed, Andy, and Brad, who followed him in.

"Unbelievable what you would…" The man stopped talking as he turned. He was tall, thin, with dark hair and thin-rimmed glasses. His hands were looped behind his back, and he was neatly dressed in a white short-sleeved dress shirt and dark blue slacks. It was the woman with him who had his stomach tightening and a sweat breaking out under his arms and down his back, sticking the light cotton of his orange collared shirt to his skin.

"Maria," he said, wondering when he'd started hating that name.

She had long hair pulled back in a ponytail, neat and tidy, a light smattering of makeup, and brown eyes that had at one time enchanted him to her innocence. But there was nothing innocent in her now.

"Neil," she said clearly in a voice he remembered. She was dressed casually in a long flowing shirt with a white camisole underneath and white cotton pants, loose and flared, gold sandals on her feet. She looked classy but did nothing for him. Her gaze drifted past him, and he had to look. His heart wept at the sight of his wife walking in and seeing the woman who was the source of her worst nightmare. He didn't want her here and wished Brad would get her out.

"I can remember a time not long ago, Maria, when you were told to leave. You were paid a lot of money to leave and not come back," Brad said, his arms crossed.

Stella had the money Neil had given to Maria in trust. That had been one of the threats to make her go away, tying up the money so she couldn't touch it if she continued to be a thorn in Neil and Candy's side and if she continued to push her interest in Michael. Yes, she was his mother by birth, but that was it. On paper, Candy was Michael's mother, and Neil feared now that this woman would always be an albatross around his neck.

"Yes, Maria, you agreed to go away. Why are you here to hassle my husband and me?" Candy said as she stepped forward.

Neil's first instinct was to step in front of Candy and ask her to go. He was about to say something to Brad, even Jed or Andy, to ask one of them to please do something here. Not for the first time, this woman had him by the balls, threatening his happily ever after, and he pictured his hands wrapped around her neck, squeezing.

"That's quite interesting coming from you, Candy. You have my son. He's not yours," Maria said. "The money is just money. You can try to threaten me again, but I've already been taken care of. Whatever you try to take away, I've made more and moved it elsewhere. I want my son." She took a step, and Mr. Pirez reached out and touched her arm.

"No," he said in a low voice.

She lowered her head and glanced down, a gold band flashing on her finger.

"You're married," Neil said just as Candy stood beside him. He wanted to reach out and touch her, slip his hand in hers, let her know his heart was tearing in two.

Maria glanced up to the older man beside her, and Neil realized that by whatever twist of fate, she had somehow met and married the man who had been about to buy his resort. It was sick. He was worried.

"What do you want?" Andy stepped forward, casually dressed in shorts and a T-shirt, but there was nothing casual about him. He was watching, assessing.

"She wants her child, Neil." Miguel Pirez spoke clearly, glancing briefly at Andy, maybe recognizing his intent or recognizing what lurked inside him that made him shrewd at what he did.

"We've been through this. You agreed. Right from the beginning, Maria, you've changed things. He's not yours. You signed your rights away. Candy is his mother, I'm his father. The adoption is final. You need to go away…"

Candy touched his arm. He wasn't sure what he saw there in her expression, but it scared the hell out of him. "Maria, you wanted my husband," she said, running her hand down Neil's arm.

Maria just watched her as her cheeks turned a hint of pink. How young she was really showed then, but she glanced down and then to her husband before looking back to Candy. "Maybe so, but I have a husband, and the child—"

"Michael," Candy interrupted.

"Michael is my son. I carried him, I gave birth to him. I changed my mind. I want to see him, to hold him, to know him."

"Neil, give me your cell phone." Candy faced him, and for the life of him, he didn't know what to think. Who was she thinking of calling? Maybe she saw his confusion when she whispered to him, "Trust me."

How could he not? He pulled his cell phone from his back pocket, and she tapped it on, bringing up their family photo and walking toward Maria.

"This is our family, Michael with his sister, Cat. You can see his joy, how happy he is."

Neil knew the photo she was showing. Michael was gazing at Candy with such love, and she had Michael in one arm, Cat in the other as she squatted down. Neil was behind her with his long hair, the beard before he'd shaved it off. Anyone could see the love there.

Candy swiped her finger over the screen. There would be piles of photos of the kids, and every one of them included Candy. These were her children. The kindness she was showing Maria had him questioning how he'd handled everything.

"He is loved," Candy said.

Neil didn't know what to make of what he was seeing as a tear slid down Maria's cheek. She held on to his phone, staring at the image on the screen, and Candy just stood there with the woman he despised, the woman who'd done the despicable thing of trying to come between Neil and his wife.

CHAPTER 32

There was soft music in the background and voices drifting in from the dining room and patio. Neil was holding a bottle of red he'd pulled from the wine cellar and was about to open it and pour a glass, just sit in the living room and make sense of everything.

He squeezed the corkscrew and set it down on the sofa table along with the bottle of wine and stepped over to the french doors, which were now closed and looked out onto the driveway. He still couldn't believe that his wife had accomplished out of an act of kindness what he'd tried to do with bullying, pleading, lying, and bribing, all with a woman who'd turned the tables on him.

He was in awe. Andy had been speechless, Brad admiring, and Jed quiet, watching as if trying to understand why and how. Maybe the women understood better, as Emily and Diana had hugged Candy. Laura, too, had seemed supportive. No one had said anything else when Maria left with her husband.

"Hey, you. I was wondering where you went off to," Becky said. She was wearing flowing cotton slacks and a T-shirt and appeared happier than he'd seen her in a long time. She didn't hesitate to reach up and run her fingers over his freshly shaven face and his longish hair. He was tempted to keep the look once again.

"Heard what happened with Maria showing up. Sounds like it really threw you for a loop." His mom listened to people and understood so much.

"My wife is smart, smarter than me. Here I have this degree and all that education, and she just handled a situation that had become my worst nightmare." He shut his eyes and shook his head, reliving the feeling that he could have lost everything, the love of his life. He looked over at his mom. "I kept thinking, why wouldn't she go away? I paid her the money, I threatened, I flexed my muscles. So did Stella, and I had my brothers and Andy with me the last time, and she still came back and was willing to toss everything away." Maybe he still didn't understand. "And my wife pulled the rug right out from under me by—"

"By being kind to a woman who nearly destroyed her. Humbling, isn't it?" His mom was smiling up at him.

"More than you know," he said, because he was still reeling over his wife's kindness and the fact that she wasn't angry at him. Maybe that was the hardest part of all. He'd created the mess, and she was being the bigger person.

"I doubt that," Becky said. "I've just lived longer, had time to do all my screw ups and learn from them. You know what the difference is, Neil, between a truly successful person and someone who isn't?"

He wasn't sure what his mom was getting at, so he shrugged as she smiled at him.

"One has made mistakes, lots, and horrible ones, but has learned and become a better person from them. He's moved on and let it go. To be a success, you have to have suffered, to understand it."

"So you found him," Candy said as she stepped down into the living room, her long dark hair hanging straight. She was wearing a lovely deep blue skirt, a matching tank top, and sandals. She was smiling, and her eyes held nothing but love for him. He wanted to weep as his mom patted his arm.

"I did. I'll leave you with him, but don't be too long. Diana and Jed have something they want to share with everyone."

He didn't miss the moment between his mom and Candy, the love in that simple touch, the connection of something shared. His wife understood so much more than he did.

"You okay?" She was staring up at him as if she wasn't sure what his reaction would be.

"I should be asking you that. I'm just…I didn't know what to do, and you walked in and…how did you know to show her photos?" He hadn't been able to figure out that proof was all she'd needed, that simple thing.

"She's a mother. Her heart was breaking, and there was nothing you could threaten her with that was going to make her go away. She just needed someone to show her kindness, no matter what she did, and to see Michael, how happy he is. I know I couldn't step in and take that from a child. It's wondering whether he's happy, whether he's loved, whether he's being taken care of and is so important to his parents that he'd never be an afterthought." Candy shrugged. "Those pictures, Neil, show our family, our love, the love we have for our children."

"And you think she'll go away now and leave us alone?" Neil had so many doubts.

"I don't know for sure. We can only hope," she said, sounding so confident.

"You're so amazing. You blew me away here, and I went apeshit last night, throwing you down—"

"For the best sex, to make me understand how much you love me."

He had to smile at her comeback. It had been all that and much more. If she only knew where his thoughts had gone. "It was rough, but I was so jealous I couldn't think straight, and you went in right up to Maria and handled it…"

"With love" she said, looking at him, letting her love shine out for him.

He reached out and skimmed his hand over her cheek, taking in the woman he was committed to, who was so much a part of him, the better part of him.

She nudged him, smiling. "Let's go and join everyone," she said, and she linked her fingers with his as she started up the steps before he stopped her.

"Hey, I just wanted to tell you, too, that Andy found us a new general manager, and he and Laura are going to stay here for a bit to help get things settled and running smoothly. Brad, Jed, Andy, and I are going to take turns coming down, but most things we can run from home once we get a system set up."

She squeezed his hand, still smiling. "I know. It's good, Neil. It will be fine."

"How do you always know it'll work out?" he asked her as they walked through the kitchen and out to the patio where everyone was.

"Because everything always does. It just doesn't happen the way we plan, and you have to be okay with that," she said, pulling him along, leaving him to think about all she'd said and done.

"It's about time you joined us," Jed called out as the

others laughed. The kids were playing on the grass. It was alive. It was family.

"Diana and I have something to share with you all," Jed said, pulling Diana up, holding her, and pressing his hand to her belly, which was a little rounded.

"She's pregnant," Brad called out. His mom reached over and smacked his arm.

"How did you know?" Diana said, sounding as if the surprise had been ruined.

"We already knew, Diana," Andy said from where Laura was sitting on his lap. "It's the glow you have."

"And it's just something we know," Brad added. Rodney waved his hand at Brad and laughed, and Neil winked at Diana as everyone congratulated them. He hung back a second until Candy had hugged her and it was his turn. He looked down at his vibrant, beautiful sister-in-law and the love she had for Jed.

"Just remember, Diana, you are beautiful, talented, a wonderful mother, and you can have it all."

Maybe that was what she'd needed to hear, because her eyes became a little misty. "Thank you, Neil, and thank you for bringing the family together." She gestured around at all of them.

Then Jed reached for his wife and pulled her into his arms as Candy, smiling and laughing, reached for Emily, and they pulled Laura up with them. These were their women, their family. They were such lucky men.

Turn the page for a sneak peek of
THE DECISION the next book in *THE FRIESSENS*
Available in print, audio & eBook.

The Friessens, stars of the bestselling series, are back with **THE DECISION**, another heartwarming fan favorite romance from **New York Times and USA Today bestselling author Lorhainne Eckhart.**

Emily Friessen has everything a woman could want: a husband who's the love of her life, a family that stands together, and children she wouldn't trade for anything. To everyone around her, she's confident and strong—but then, she has to be with a man like Brad, who is all about family and too handsome for his own good.

Emily isn't as together as she appears, though, and when life throws her and Brad a curveball, it tests their relationship, leaving Emily scrambling and feeling very much alone as both are faced with a decision no parent should have to make.

CHAPTER 1

Brad walked the ridge overlooking his land, taking in the browns and golds of the drying pasture to the tree line, where the forest thickened and thinned closer to the many outbuildings, big and small, on his ranch—a ranch that had been in his family for generations. This was Friessen land, and being the eldest son to Rodney Friessen, he had inherited everything. At the time, Brad had never questioned how only he, the eldest of three, could have all this. That was what happened in families: The eldest son inherited the earth. Was that not the saying?

His brother Jed, the youngest, had been left to set out on his own and had bought a piece of shit property in Snohomish County, where he had built something from nothing. Jed was pigheaded, at times so closed off that Brad wondered what he was thinking, but he loved him. He loved all his family. His father had retired down in Cancun, having bought a huge ranching operation on the Yucatan Peninsula with his brother Neil, a Harvard graduate who owned a multimillion-dollar resort. Brad, meanwhile, had been handed all of this, and at times he wondered whether he had earned any of it. Yes, he worked hard, but he'd never had to work to gain something, to create something.

He'd never considered himself fortunate or privileged. He'd never thought much of it until recently. Maybe it was age, becoming older and wiser. He smiled to himself, wondering, if it were possible, would he go back and change anything, trade in all the pain, the heartache…and the love he had now? No, he supposed he wouldn't. All the choices he'd made, both good and bad, had brought him here. They had brought him Emily, their children, and a life filled with struggles. It had been a bumpy road, but he wouldn't trade his family for anything. He had everything he could ever want.

Being a rancher, one could say, was in his blood. He didn't want to do anything else. He was a part owner of his brother's fancy resort in Cancun, but, as he'd said to Neil, as long as he didn't have to take part in the daily operations, that was fine with him. There was one thing Brad understood and knew deep down that many people didn't, something people struggled and searched for their entire lives. This was where he belonged, on this fertile rock in the Pacific Northwest, with his land. The only problem was that Angus Friessen, his grandfather, being old, Irish, and proud of it, had added an addendum on the property that it could only pass to the eldest son—not the daughter! What the man had been thinking was beyond Brad. Considering times had changed, it seemed over the top even to him.

He realized, as he took in the vast acreage, with a spectacular view of the pastures below, the grazing cattle, the field of hay, and his horses, that having a male heir was going to be a problem, as his son, his only son, had autism.

He took a deep breath, seeing his ranch hands and a

dusty trail in the distance. He had to squint to see who was coming, but then, it was late afternoon. The kids would be home soon. It had to be the school bus pulling in. Trevor, Katy, and Becky, his youngest, would be racing down the driveway and turning their once quiet house into a lively affair for Emily. With only a few weeks left until the end of the school year, they needed to have a heart to heart about what was next for Trevor. Emily had already mentioned it four times. (Brad had heard her the first time, but she'd needed to repeat herself because he hadn't replied.)

Trevor would be seventeen soon, and the girls were growing up fast, too. From Emily's first marriage, Katy was a year younger than Trevor and was blond and slender, with a young lady's figure that was turning the heads of a few young boys, who were calling all the time. It was giving Brad a few gray hairs as he considered, now, how to handle his girls. It was time he and Emily sat Katy down and laid out the rules for dating. Of course, he wouldn't hesitate to put the fear of God into each and every one of those boys who came knocking. Becky, their little girl, was just entering her teenage years. He'd already noticed the change in attitude, as she was giving Emily more lip than before, testing her boundaries. He needed to have a chat with her, too.

Maybe that was why he'd spent the last week walking the ridgeline, looking over the property as he did his best to get his head on straight and figure out what was next. He felt for the first time that they were fast wading into the new and different territory of raising two teenage girls and a young autistic man. What to do? Tonight he'd take Emily aside and they'd make some decisions about what was next for their family.

And this land.

He took in the trail he'd climbed up and slung his rifle

over his shoulder just as his cell phone rang. He reached for it from his back pocket and saw "Home" displayed there, smiling because Emily was probably wondering where he'd gone off to. "On my way," he started.

"Dad!" Katy cried out in a tone that had the hair standing up on the back of his neck.

"Whoa, what's going on?"

"It's Trevor, Dad. Mom said to call you and get you back here. Someone hurt him…" She was starting to ramble on and heading toward hysterics, and he couldn't understand a word she was saying.

"Katy, stop it, calm down. I'm heading back to the house." He was running down the trail, sliding sideways in spots with the phone to his ear. "How bad is he hurt? Put your mom on!" He knew he was shouting, but he couldn't do a damn thing, being this far from the house, and that made him furious.

"I can't put Mom on. She has Trevor upstairs. She's trying to stop the bleeding. It's horrible, Dad." He could hear the edge in her voice, and of course his head was going to some pretty bad places.

This was one of those times, as he broke the tree line, that he wanted to kick himself in the ass for not saddling a horse. "Did she call an ambulance?"

There was silence for a minute.

"Katy!" Brad yelled into the phone as he waved in the air to Cliff, who was on the tractor, but then thought better of it. He started running toward the house, pounding the ground, his rifle over his shoulder.

"No," Katy said, sounding confused.

In that second, as he got closer to the house, he realized something wasn't quite right.

"Why not?" he said into the phone as he raced up the back steps, hanging up the phone and seeing Katy in the kitchen, standing and holding the phone to her ear. "Em!" He shouted as he took in Katy, pale, wide eyed, looking to him and then the phone and then hanging it up. He was out of breath, sweating as he rested his hand on her shoulder. Just then, there was a squeak on the stairs.

"Daddy!" Becky raced down. "You should see all the blood from Trevor." She seemed excited and impressed, and Brad wanted answers.

"Brad, up here! Emily said. "Trevor has a nose bleed."

Seriously? He glared down at Katy, who was standing there and shrugging. "A nose bleed," he said. "We're going to have a talk later about your dramatics."

He walked to the back door, opened the gun cabinet, and unloaded the rifle before setting it back in, locking the cabinet up, and putting the key in his pocket. He started up the stairs and into the bathroom, where Trevor was holding a wet cloth to his nose. There was blood on his yellow T-shirt, but he appeared far from hurt.

"Hi, Dad," he said in a nasal tone, smiling as he pulled the cloth away. His nose was still dripping and appeared a little pink but not swollen. Otherwise he looked fine.

"What's going on here? I get this panicked call from Katy that Trevor is hurt, was beat up or something bad, and she made it sound as if he needed to go to Emergency."

Emily had spots of fresh blood on her sleeveless pale blue shirt, her brown hair pinned up in a messy bun. She raised an eyebrow, shaking her head. "No, I didn't get the whole story from Katy, though, as she pulled Trevor in, both her and Becky. All they said was that he'd been hurt on the bus. I told her to call you and get you back here so we could find out who we need to hunt down." She sounded really mad, and he could see she was probably jumping to conclusions, considering they weren't getting the entire story.

"Girls, get up here!" Brad called out. "Trevor, what happened?"

"I fell," he said, then looked in the mirror as if studying his nose.

"What is it?" Katy appeared with her sister behind her. They were both staring at Trevor.

"Katy, I didn't tell you to call your dad and scare him, making him think the worst had happened with Trevor. I don't understand why you'd do that."

She shrugged. "Sorry, but it was a lot of blood, Mom. Even you were worried when you saw it."

"It was really gross," Becky added.

"We're going to talk later about that, Katy, but right now I want to know what happened here. Trevor, you said you fell?" Brad rested his hand on Trevor's shoulder as Emily leaned in, fussing again, dabbing at his nose with another cloth.

"Katy tripped me."

"I did not trip you, Trevor!" she yelled out, sounding truly affronted.

"Oops, sorry, my mistake," he said and laughed.

"It was Deanna Miller. She's in grade twelve. I saw her stick her foot out when Trevor went past, and she tripped him. She's not very nice," Becky said. "I heard her talking with that awful Jason Cresswell, saying they needed to take down the idiot."

Brad was trying to figure out who these kids were, and he found himself looking to Emily and then over to Katy. He was stuck on the "idiot" part. What kid would say something so hurtful, so wrong?

"It's okay," Trevor said, putting the washcloth in the hamper.

"No, it's not okay, Trevor," Brad said. "If someone hurt you, you have to say something. Tell us, did this Deanna trip you?"

Trevor just shrugged. "I don't know."

"Dad, I was ahead of Trevor when he fell," Katy said. "I didn't see it, but Deanna is not nice. Trevor, you shouted when you fell. I helped you up, and you were holding your nose, and there was blood pouring out. I heard the bus driver asking all the kids what happened when we got off."

"She was really mad," Becky added.

"Who is Jason Cresswell? I don't think I know him," Emily said. Trevor was now looking in the mirror, examining the side of his nose.

"He's in grade eleven. He's a bully. I don't like him," Becky said.

"I think maybe I need to go and have a talk with the school," Emily said.

"How about, since we're not rushing off to the emergency room now and everyone appears to be okay, you go work on your homework?" Brad said to the kids. "I'm going to have a talk with your mom."

"I don't have homework, Dad," Becky said.

"I don't have homework, either," Trevor announced.

Katy was frowning. "That's so not fair. Why do I have to have it all piled on me? Trevor never gets anything." She was crossing her arms as if she wanted to argue her point.

"That's because he has autism," Becky added with dramatics, rolling her eyes.

"Okay, enough. Katy, go do your homework," Emily said. "I know you haven't finished that book report you were supposed to do. Oh, yes, I got an email today from your teacher. Becky, go read a book. Trevor, you too." She took a breath, sounding as if she was nearing the end of her rope.

Brad took in the large main bathroom with its dated tub and shower. "So, sounds like we have a problem with some kids picking on Trevor," he said. Emily turned and stared at him, firming her lips, appearing frustrated as she walked out of the bathroom and into their large master suite. Brad followed, closing the door behind him as Emily pulled off the bloody shirt and tossed it in with the dirty clothes. She lifted a peach T-shirt out of their six-drawer chest and pulled it on.

"You're not answering me now," he said. He couldn't believe she'd walked away from him, and he was trying to figure out what was going through her head when she turned around and stumbled a bit.

"Em!" He reached her before she fell, lifting her in his arms, resting her on the bed. She was pale and had an odd look on her face as she widened her eyes and blinked.

When she looked up at him, she said, "I'm pregnant."

ABOUT THE AUTHOR

"Lorhainne Eckhart is one of my go to authors when I want a guaranteed good book. So many twists and turns, but also so much love and such a strong sense of family."

— (LORA W., REVIEWER)

New York Times & USA Today bestseller Lorhainne Eckhart writes Raw Relatable Real Romance is best known for her big family romances series, where "Morals and family are running themes. Danger, romance, and a drive to do what is right will see you glued to the page." As one fan calls her, she is the "Queen of the family saga." (aherman) writing "the ups and downs of what goes on within a family but also with some suspense, angst and of course a bit of romance thrown in for good measure." Follow Lorhainne on Bookbub to receive alerts on New Releases and Sales and join her mailing list at LorhainneEckhart.com for her Monday Blog, books news, giveaways and FREE reads. With over 120 books, audiobooks, and multiple series published and available at all retailers now translated into six languages. She is a multiple recipient of the Readers' Favorite Award for Suspense and Romance, and lives in the Pacific Northwest on an island, is the mother of three, her oldest has autism and she is an advocate for never giving up on your dreams.

"Lorhainne Eckhart has this uncanny way of just hitting the spot every time with her books."

— (CAROLINE L., REVIEWER)

The O'Connells: *The O'Connells of Livingston, Montana are not your typical family. A riveting collection of stories surrounding the ups and downs of what goes on within a family but also with some suspense, angst and of course a bit of romance thrown in for good measure "I thought I loved the Friessens, but I absolutely adore the O'Connell's. Each and every book has totally different genres of stories but the one thing in common is how she is able to wrap it around the family which is the heart of each story." (C. Logue)*

The Friessens: *An emotional big family romance series, the Friessen family siblings find their relationships tested, lay their hearts on the*

line, and discover lasting love! "Lorhainne
Eckhart is one of my go to authors when I want
a guaranteed good book. So many twists and
turns, but also so much love and such a strong
sense of family." (Lora W., Reviewer)

The Parker Sisters: The Parker Sisters are a
close-knit family, and like any other family they
have their ups and downs. "Eckhart has crafted
another intense family drama…The character
development is outstanding, and the emotional
investment is high…" (Aherman, Reviewer)

The McCabe Brothers: Join the five
McCabe siblings on their journeys to the dark
and dangerous side of love! An intense, exhila-
rating collection of romantic thrillers you won't
want to miss. — "Eckhart has a new series
that is definitely worth the read. The queen of
the family saga started this series with a spin-
off of her wildly successful Friessen series."
From a Readers' Favorite award—winning
author and "queen of the family saga"
(Aherman)

Lorhainne loves to hear from her readers! You can connect with me at:
www.LorhainneEckhart.com
lorhainneeckhart.le@gmail.com

In the Silence
In the Charm
Unexpected Consequences
It Was Always You
The First Time I Saw You
Welcome to My Arms
Welcome to Boston
I'll Always Love You
Ground Rules
A Reason to Breathe
You Are My Everything
Anything For You
The Homecoming
Stay Away From My Daughter
The Bad Boy
A Place of Our Own
The Visitor
All About Devon
Long Past Dawn
How to Heal a Heart
Keep Me in Your Heart

The O'Connells
The Neighbor
The Third Call
The Secret Husband
The Quiet Day
The Commitment
The Missing Father
The Hometown Hero
Justice
The Family Secret
The Fallen O'Connell
The Return of the O'Connells

And The She Was Gone
The Stalker
The O'Connell Family Christmas
The Girl Next Door
Broken Promises
The Gatekeeper

The McCabe Brothers
Don't Stop Me (Vic)
Don't Catch Me (Chase)
Don't Run From Me (Aaron)
Don't Hide From Me (Luc)
Don't Leave Me (Claudia)
Out of Time

A Billy Jo McCabe Mystery
Nothing As it Seems
Hiding in Plain Sight
The Cold Case
The Trap
Above the Law
The Stranger at the Door
The Children
The Last Stand
The Charity

The Street Fighter
Finding Home

The Wilde Brothers
The One (Joe and Margaret)
The Honeymoon, A Wilde Brothers Short
Friendly Fire (Logan and Julia)
Not Quite Married, A Wilde Brothers Short

A Matter of Trust (Ben and Carrie)
The Reckoning, A Wilde Brothers Christmas
Traded (Jake)
Unforgiven (Samuel)
The Holiday Bride

Married in Montana
His Promise
Love's Promise
A Promise of Forever

The Parker Sisters
Thrill of the Chase
The Dating Game
Play Hard to Get
What We Can't Have
Go Your Own Way
A June Wedding

Kate & Walker
One Night
Edge of Night
Last Night

Walk the Right Road Series
The Choice
Lost and Found
Merkaba
Bounty
Blown Away: The Final Chapter

The Saved Series
Saved
Vanished

Captured

Single Titles
He Came Back
Loving Christine

For my German Readers
Die Außenseiter-Reihe
Der Vergessene Junge
Der Gefallene Held

For my French Readers
L'ENFANT OUBLIÉ

www.ingramcontent.com/pod-product-compliance
Lightning Source LLC
Chambersburg PA
CBHW030941210726
48290CB00007B/2283